VIRAGO
MODERN CLASSICS
726

Noel Streatfeild was born on Christmas Eve, 1895, in Sussex. After working in munitions factories and canteens for the armed forces during the First World War, Noel followed her dream of being on stage and went to the Royal Academy of Dramatic Art, becoming a professional actress.

Streatfeild began writing children's books in 1931 and her most famous novel, *Ballet Shoes*, was published in 1936. She quickly became one of the most popular authors of her day. She was one of the first winners of the Carnegie Medal and was awarded an OBE in 1983.

Available in Virago Children's Classics

NOEL STREATFEILD'S Holiday Stories

With illustrations by Peter Bailey

VIRAGO

This collection first published in Great Britain in 2019 by Virago Press
This paperback edition published in 2022 by Virago Press

13 5 7 9 10 8 6 4 2

A CIP catalogue record for this book is available from the British Library.

ISBN 978-0-349-01096-0

Typeset in Goudy by M Rules
Printed and bound in Great Britain by Clays Ltd, Elcograf S.p.A.

Papers used by Virago are from well-managed forests
and other responsible sources.

MIX
Paper from
responsible sources
FSC® C104740

Virago Press
An imprint of
Little, Brown Book Group
Carmelite House
50 Victoria Embankment
London EC4Y 0DZ

An Hachette UK Company
www.hachette.co.uk

www.virago.co.uk

Contents

The Plain One: A Note from the Author

Although it never seems like it at the time, there is a lot to be said for not being a too glamorous and successful child. The kind of child – and this applies especially to girls – who never goes through a plain patch, about whom everybody says 'Isn't she sweet?' or 'Isn't she a darling?', and who consistently does well at school, can have a much harder time finding her feet when she grows up than the less successful.

I write from experience. We were three sisters in my family and I was the middle one and plain. My eldest sister was pretty, talented and, in spite of being delicate, exceedingly good at school work. My younger sister was not just pretty, she was beautiful – the sort of child at whom people stop and stare – and she was sharp as a needle at school.

I, in the middle, was what is now called 'a slow developer'. I was not really an ugly child but, compared to the other two, I was downright plain. Nobody ever discovered why I stubbornly refused to work at school. My teachers never had the slightest doubt that I could do well if I would try but I just wouldn't try. As a result I was nagged day and night until I got what was called in nursery parlance 'a black dog on my shoulder'. I took to scowling and growling and the more I scowled and growled the less lovable I became.

But, for a writer, especially if they are going to write either for or about children, this rather black-doggish childhood is a well of information. Being an unsuccessful child makes you look very carefully, with almost grown-up eyes, at yourself and the people around you. You try to assess why you are being a failure. For instance, you may think your parents don't love you as much as they love the others. (This is, of course, totally untrue. They probably love you more because you need more help.) At the same time you observe your sisters and brothers and work out for yourself the reason why they can glide so easily through childhood while you do so much stumbling. Then there are the other children that you meet. In most families the unsuccessful child can discern a fellow spirit who also is perhaps the plainest of the family and does the least well at school.

When I grew up and started to write books I found to my great surprise that always studying children when I was a child myself had stayed with me and I only had to look back into my childhood to see the sort of things that children do and why. That is the reason why in my books there are often plain children who get into more trouble than the rest of the family. You see, I can remember what it was like.

I would not like those of you who are pretty and wonderfully successful at school to think this is going to be a disadvantage to you. Of course it isn't – but remember this was written by the plain one of the family.

Devon Mettle

Staying with Grandmother was an event, the loveliest bit of the summer, a glorious time. It had happened every year since John was nine months old and Barbara not there at all. But this year was better than all the other years, for they were sent alone. Not actually for the railway part, for Daddy had been with them for that, but he had gone back the next day and left them with Granny and old Hannah, which meant they weren't looked after at all. For Granny had the most sensible ideas about what children might do. 'Go where you like,' she would say, 'you are as safe on a Devonshire moor as in your bed.' But she always extracted a promise from them before they started out. 'Now, you must never lose sight of my cottage. I wish for your promise, my dears.' They found the promise an easy one to keep, for the cottage was in a valley, and they could climb up the hills and on to the moor for quite a long way in every direction and still see the thatch on the roof and the big slash of colour made by the hollyhocks.

One lazy, stuffy afternoon Hannah brought to them two baskets.

'Look here, go up on the moor now, my dears, and pick me some whorts. I hear they're beautiful.'

The children had often picked whortleberries before, and they thought it fun even when escorted by Nurse, but alone it seemed an important thing to be asked to do. They snatched up their hats and started for the door, but Granny called them back.

'Are you going to pick me some whortleberries?' The children nodded. 'Then I shall want two promises today, the usual one, and a new one. I wish you only to eat ten berries each, for unless they are stewed they are apt to be very upsetting. Besides, you will enjoy them better served with my thick cream.'

The sun was blazing down on the moor and before the children reached the place where the whortleberries grew, their legs were tired with pushing through the heather, and their arms with brushing aside the bracken.

'Let's sit a minute,' Barbara panted. She stretched her legs out comfortably in front of her. 'Heather's lovely stuff to sit on, all springy like that sofa at home.'

'I wonder if it hurts it, being sat on.' John rolled over on to his tummy to stare at the plant beneath him. 'I expect it can't like it much.'

'Well we won't sit on those bits very long.' Barbara gave her plant a comforting pat. 'In a minute we'll move on and sit on other plants instead.'

The whortleberries were growing in masses. They were pleasantly easy to pick, and for a while both children worked industriously. Then Barbara paused and with purple fingers regretfully put her tenth berry into her already purple mouth. She looked at John's busy back view.

'How many have you eaten?'

'Well, only eight really, but I've sucked some squashed ones off my fingers, I don't think Granny would count those.'

'I bet she would, I bet she'd count them as halves.'

'Halves!' John went rigid with contempt. 'Halves! Don't be so silly, why often they're only one lick.'

Barbara looked severe.

'Well, four squashed ones shall count as one whole one, but it isn't fair really, I know your licks.'

John accepted this, and for a while worked on, then he straightened himself.

'I've picked thousands and thousands,' he grunted, for the picking position led to grunts.

Barbara stood upright too, and pushed the hair out of her eyes, leaving purple streaks on her forehead, then suddenly she stiffened and her face slowly flooded with crimson.

'Oh! We've come too far. We can't see Granny's.'

John studied the landscape, then he too flushed, for a promise is a promise.

'We'd better go back.'

They turned about and set off hurriedly in the opposite direction, but crouching along picking, it's very difficult to notice which way you are going. The children soon found they hadn't noticed at all, then the bracken grew so thick and tall it seemed to hide things, and the faster they tried to go the more the heather seemed to cling to their feet.

'It can't have gone really,' said Barbara without much conviction. Her lip quivered.

'Of course it can't, silly.'

It was then that they stumbled upon the man. He was

lying so flat upon the ground that they almost fell over him. He seemed as startled by the encounter as they were, and spoke roughly.

'What do you want?'

'Nothing,' said John in a brave voice, though he wasn't really feeling it.

'We're lost,' Barbara explained.

'Lost!' The man looked up at her mouth, and down at her fingers and smiled suddenly. It was an odd smile which seemed to come from far down inside him, and not to happen often. 'Lost picking whortleberries.'

'Yes, that's it.' Barbara sat down beside him happily. She was delighted they had found him, he was a grown-up, and from such all knowledge was to be expected, including the way home. 'Have you been picking them too?'

'No, there aren't any just hereabouts.'

'But there are lots a little further on.'

'I know, but I like it here where the bracken's thick.' Then he added inconsequently, 'Kind stuff bracken.'

'Is it! That's all you know.' John held out a cut finger. 'A bit I tried to pick did this to me. I wanted it for swatting flies.'

The man nodded gravely.

'Oh yes, it cuts, but it shelters too.'

'Yes, it does,' Barbara agreed. 'Last year when we were up here with Nurse it rained and rained so we all lay on a rug under the bracken, and when it got fine we weren't hardly wet at all.'

'And Granny was waiting for us at the gate when we got back because she thought we'd have been almost drowned,' John added. 'And she was awfully surprised to find us all dry, for the garden path was flooded, but it floods very easily, you know.'

The man sat up when John finished speaking, and stared at him.

'The garden path was flooded, it floods very easily.' He spoke in an odd far-away voice as if he was remembering things. When he spoke again it was almost angrily in a demanding sort of way.

'Where does your grandmother live?'

'In the valley.' Barbara waved her arm vaguely towards the horizon.

'Stack Cottage, it's called,' John explained.

'Stack Cottage! Stack Cottage!' the man whispered. 'And the boy speaks of it in his ordinary voice; doesn't he know he speaks of holy ground?' He looked first at one child and then at the other and saw they were puzzled and a little frightened. He grinned at them. 'Don't mind me, I'm a sentimental old fool, but tell me, is there still an apple tree just inside the gate?'

'Oh yes.' John settled down comfortably again now they were back talking of normal things. 'We call that our tree because we are allowed to eat those apples without asking.'

'So was I.' The man lay back amongst the bracken fronds, and stared at the sky. Barbara took a large whortleberry out of her basket, turned it over longingly, gave it a small lick, and regretfully put it back.

'Did you live at Granny's once?'

'I did, though it wasn't your grandmother's then, it belonged to my father, and I was born there, and lived there till I was fourteen. I used to ride over every inch of this moor.'

'Ride!' The children looked at him enviously.

'You were lucky,' John grumbled. 'I don't ride, they always say about me, "Not worth getting the boy a pony for the short time he's here".'

'And I learned to throw my first fly in that stretch of river that runs at the bottom of the garden.'

John aimed a stick savagely at a plant of willowherb.

'We aren't allowed to go near the river, it frightens Mummy.'

'Not nearer than the last rose-tree unless somebody's with us,' Barbara added, but the man didn't seem to be listening; he was gazing at the hillside opposite, looking very queer indeed. She thought perhaps he was feeling miserable, so she patted his arm comfortingly. 'You needn't worry about the cottage, Granny looks after it very nicely, and so does Hannah.'

The pat had focused his attention.

'I'm sure they do.' He said no more but continued to stare dreamily at the hills, so dreamily that John was afraid he was going to sleep, and since his help was urgently needed he gave him a little nudge.

'Do you think you remember the way to the cottage?'

'You see, we ought not really to be where we can't see it.' Barbara spoke earnestly. 'So if you could show us the way—'

'Show you the way!' The man looked startled. 'Oh my dears, I can't, you don't know what you're asking.'

'Just a little way,' Barbara urged. 'Couldn't you?'

'I could, but it's such short scrubby stuff further down, just heather, and perhaps a few whortleberries.' He looked pleadingly at her. 'You're not really asking me to leave my bracken, are you?'

'Just to show us the way, you needn't come far. Besides, if there are whortleberries you could eat some as we go, they're awfully nice.' Then she looked at his odd shabby clothes, perhaps he was worrying about them. 'The stain won't get all over you like it has us. We sat on them, you know. Besides, if one does get stuck on you, often it will come off for just one suck, and never leave a mark.'

The man laughed.

'Bless my soul, I'm not worrying about these clothes.' He looked down at himself bitterly. 'But you don't know what you ask. There are people in the valley I don't want to meet.'

'Well, let's crawl like we do when we scout,' John suggested.

'Crawl! Crawl!' The man sprang to his feet and flung out his chest, and threw back his head in one supreme gesture. 'Crawl!' he roared again. 'Would you see a Devon man crawl to his own home? Never! Give me your hands.' He gripped John's paw in one large fist and Barbara's in the other, and set off down the hill at a terrific pace, and as he swung along he broke into a song with a rollicking chorus which helped the children's feet to hurry:

> *'While the raging seas did roar,*
> *And the stormy winds did blow,*
> *While we jolly sailor-boys went skipping to*
> *   the top,*
> *And the land-lubbers lying down below, below,*
> *   below,*
> *And the land-lubbers lying down below.'*

'Well, how did you like that?' he asked when he had finished.

'Very much,' panted Barbara politely. 'But I'm sorry they were all drowned. They were, weren't they?'

He looked down at her, and slowed up as he saw how out of breath he had made her.

'There are worse things than drowning.'

'But they were dead.'

'There are many worse things than death.'

'I'd hate to drown, though,' John objected.

'Hate to, but not fear to, or you are no Devon man. No Devon man ever feared the sea. We've history to prove it.'

'You mean people like Drake?' John suggested.

'And many others. But Drake! Oh, there was a man, there was a fellow to follow. He feared no element and no man, and knew how to scotch a snake when he met one.'

John was interested.

'Did Drake kill snakes? I never knew that.'

'One he did, a thing called Doughty, he strung him to the yard-arm.'

'Did he?' John was silent, visualising rows of slaughtered snakes hung so, and missed the man's whisper.

'He was his best friend too, but he was honoured for what he did. Ah! they understood men then.'

They came to a sudden small rise and below them lay the cottage. The man loosed their hands, and laid his upon their shoulders.

'There it is, run to it, you lucky little devils.'

'Goodbye,' John said politely.

'Thank you very much,' Barbara added.

The man gave them an affectionate push.

'Scoot! Oh and by the way, John, if ever you meet a snake, don't be afraid to kill it.'

That evening when the children were in bed, Hannah came into the drawing-room and stood in front of Grandmother.

'Well, Hannah?'

'They've caught an escaped convict.'

'Where?'

'Up on the moor anigh this very house. They've been searching all day, but could not tell the way he went. Then sudden-like he left the bracken where he were lyin' and came out in the open for all to see, which were foolishness I reckon. And who do you think the convict were? Why, young Maister Gordon, son of old Maister who lived here before you, mum.'

'Why was he sent to prison?'

'He was a murderer. He killed his best friend, who stole away his wife.'

'Why was he not hanged?'

'He's been lucky, I reckon.'

'A murderer here on our moor!' The colour faded from Grandmother's cheeks. 'How terrible.'

Hannah jerked her thumb upwards to the children's rooms.

'They're safe and snug, they saw naught of he.'

Grandmother bent her head, her lips moved, then she said softly:

'We have much to thank God for. Fetch me my Prayer Book, I should like to read the hundred and fiftieth Psalm.'

Chicken for Supper

Just as if it made no difference to anybody, Canon Bell said:

'I've asked our Member of Parliament to supper on Sunday, Cathy.'

Mrs Bell, though they had been married for years, had never got used to his unpractical ideas about everyday things.

'Oh, Alex! Not Sunday! What is he to eat?'

Mrs Gage, because she had 'done' the Vicarage so long, took part by right in any family discussion.

'Oh, you never, Canon! Sunday! Member of

Parliament. You'll be givin' the Lord Mayor an invite next.' Then she turned soothingly to Cathy. 'We'll manage, dear. I'll send Mr Gage out so I can give you a 'and.'

The children asked questions. Paul why the MP was coming. Jane what he was like. Ginnie if it would mean a proper party supper. Angus, if it was a party supper, if he and Ginnie might stay up for it.

Canon Bell explained that the MP was called Mr Billet, he was rich, and spent part of his money on playing-fields; he thought one was needed near St Mark's and was coming to supper to discuss the idea. He would not expect a banquet in a vicarage on a Sunday evening, but he would, of course, have the best they could afford. Then Alex looked at the clock, said he was late, and hurried out.

Mrs Gage looked after him with a very expressive face. 'These men! Best we can afford! As if 'e didn't know Sunday supper's always been what's left of the Sunday joint, with a dish of beets, and some potatoes. Never mind, Mrs Bell dear, we'll think up somethin' posh.'

Mrs Gage thought up a chicken. About two miles from St Mark's Vicarage there was a Sunday street market. One of the stallholders there was a distant cousin of Mr Gage's.

'Ernie sells veg and that, proper shark 'e is, 'ave a bite of 'is mother if 'e was 'ungry; but Mr Gage did 'im a good turn once, so we'll make 'im cough up a big boilin' fowl, and let us 'ave it cheap.'

The cost of the chicken after much argument on the telephone was fixed at fourteen shillings.

'You're to fetch it after dinner Sunday,' Mrs Gage told the children. 'Ernie says 'e don't want you while the market's on, but 'e's got some business after so 'e won't be movin' 'is barrow till the afternoon.'

It was not only that Sunday was an awkward day for entertaining, it happened to be a particularly inconvenient day for Mrs Bell; for she, who hardly ever went far on Sundays, was going to a special service for women in the Albert Hall. To make the day more awkward, Canon Bell too had to be away.

'You'll have to see to your own lunch, darlings,' Cathy told the children, 'and directly afterwards go and fetch the chicken.' She gave Paul a pound. 'You can buy ices with some of the change.'

Mrs Gage looked at the pound.

'Don't leave 'old of that, Paul, till you 'ave the chicken in your 'and, and don't take too long over the ices. I'll be back tea-time, for I won't be 'appy about a boiler of Ernie's till I 'ave it in the pot.'

The children had never been to the Sunday market, but they had always wanted to see it; so they and Esau, their dog, started out the moment they had washed up the lunch things.

'Oh goodness,' said Jane, 'do let's hurry. I do wish we could have gone in the morning when it's properly open. I expect it's almost finished by the afternoon.'

'There must be other people there as well as Ernie,' Paul pointed out, 'because he said he'd be doing business, so it must be with someone.'

They hurried so fast that Ginnie, who was fat, spoke in puffs: 'I bet there's some market left.'

Angus had to run a few steps to catch up.

'I hope there's a goldfish stall.'

When the children and Esau reached the market street it was clear they were too late to see much. There was a great deal of what had been a market: squashed vegetables and flowers, bits of paper, broken boxes; but very few barrows and stalls. Mrs Gage had told them that Ernie's barrow would be at the far end of the street, so they walked towards it, and that was how they found the puppy stall. First they saw a crowd of people, and then they heard little, thin, high puppy voices. Without a word said, all four pushed forward.

It was not easy to see the puppies. Angus managed by

getting down on all fours, and climbing under people's legs until he came out in the front row. Ginnie got a fair view by disgraceful pushing. Jane would not have seen a hair on a puppy's tail if Paul had not helped her. On the outside of the crowd was a big man in a check overcoat, with his hands in his pockets. Paul looked at him and put Esau on his lead:

'I'll press next to him,' he whispered, 'and make him move over, then you squeeze in and stand on tiptoe.'

The puppies were charming but rather sad. A big rough man was selling them and none of the children felt certain he cared that every puppy had a good home. All the same they would have stayed looking at them until the last one was sold if the big man in the check coat had not decided to move so suddenly that Paul nearly fell over, and this reminded him of the time.

'We must get on,' he told Jane. 'Can you shout at the others?'

Ernie's stall was not far from the puppy stall, so almost at once Paul discovered the terrible thing that had happened. His wallet had been stolen. There was no money to pay for the chicken.

Horrified the children stared at each other, while the awfulness of the situation seeped in on them.

Mummy was out. Daddy was out. They could not get another pound. Without the chicken there was no proper supper for a Member of Parliament. Ernie was merciless. He put the parcel back on his barrow.

'No money, no chicken: that's straight.'

Ginnie wanted to argue with Ernie, but Paul stopped her.

'We'll get another fourteen shillings somehow. How long can you give us?'

Ernie looked at his watch.

'I leaves 'ere four o'clock sharp.'

Jane tugged at Paul's sleeve to get him out of Ernie's hearing: 'The man in the check coat! You were pressed right against him. It must have been him. There was only me on the other side.'

In a moment all four and Esau were haring up the street; but Paul, though he too was hurrying, was doubtful.

'I don't see what we can do, I mean even if we see him we can't tell him he took it, because we're only guessing.'

But the other three would not listen.

'Who else could it be?' Jane asked.

'He's what they call a spiv,' Ginnie panted. 'On the films they always wear check coats.'

Angus was so out of breath he could scarcely get his words out.

'We'll track him to his lair.'

At the end of the street they stopped. Jane peered round a wall: in a second she jerked her head back.

'He's there, walking up the High Street.'

'Good,' said Ginnie, 'we'll shadow him.'

The High Street had a Sunday afternoon emptiness, so it was easy, without attracting attention, for the Bells to dodge from door to door. Suddenly the man turned to the left.

'Let's run,' Ginnie whispered, 'or we'll lose him.'

The man was in the next street, doing something to the bonnet of a car.

'He is a thief,' said Angus. 'That's a Bentley, I bet it isn't his.'

Paul looked worried.

'All the same, I don't see what we can do.'

'I don't know what you were planning,' said Ginnie, 'but Miss Virginia Bell is going to face him and make him give our pound back.'

Ginnie marched towards the car, and, less certainly, the others followed. They stood in a ring round the man. 'If you don't mind my saying so,' said Ginnie, 'it's a pretty mean thing to steal a pound.'

Angus joined in: 'And especially a pound that didn't belong to the people that had it, but was for buying supper for a distinguished guest.'

The man looked in an odd way at each of the Bells.

'What proof have you?'

Ginnie was going to answer rudely, but Paul spoke first. 'None. But you were next to me while I was looking at the puppies.'

'I was on the other side of him,' Jane explained, 'so there was only you.'

The man leant against the car.

'Nobody should be accused on such flimsy evidence. But to satisfy yourselves you may search me.'

Jane and Paul felt uncomfortable, but Ginnie and Angus had no such feelings. They fell on the man and turned out all his pockets, coat, jacket, and waistcoat; the result was a shock. In loose change there was about two pounds, in the wallet only one note, and that was for five pounds.

'I say, sir, I'm awfully sorry,' said Paul; 'but you do see you looked suspicious.'

Jane's face was crimson she was so ashamed. 'You seemed the only person and we hadn't time to think.'

Ginnie rebuttoned the man's overcoat and gave him a comforting pat.

'We had to be quick, the chicken man will only stay till four.'

Angus helped with the buttoning.

'And there's nothing else for the distinguished guest for supper.'

The man looked stern. 'I could have you all up for defamation of character but let's have the whole story.'

None of them knew for certain what defamation of character was, but they wanted to show the man they realised that, far from being a thief, he was a friend, so they all talked at once. The man held up his hand. He looked at Jane. 'You tell me.'

Jane still felt red all over, so her voice was rather fade-away-ish.

'Daddy, he's the vicar of St Mark's, has asked our MP, who's called Mr Billet, to supper today to talk about playing-fields ...'

Ginnie felt Jane was explaining badly.

'Which was awful news for Mummy, because we only have mimsy-pimsy suppers on Sunday.'

Angus leant against the man.

'But Mrs Gage's husband has a cousin called Ernie who has a barrow in the market where the puppies are, and he has chickens, and Mrs Gage made him sell us a boiler cheap ...'

'And the pound was to pay for the chicken?' asked the man.

'Fourteen shillings of it,' Paul explained. 'And we were to have two shillings' worth of ices.'

Jane, feeling cold all over, remembered how desperate the position was. 'It's simply too awful: we can't get another pound because Mummy and Daddy are out, and Mr Billet will only have our lunch leave-overs, imagine the shame!'

The man looked shocked. 'Terrible!' He paused to

think. 'You all realise how wrong you were to accuse somebody of stealing without a shred of evidence?'

The family nodded. Ginnie said:

'We were loathsome worms, but we were so fussed.'

The man nodded.

'That being so I might help you, but there is a condition. I'll go with you to Ernie and pay for the chicken, but I shall call at St Mark's this evening for my money. I want you to promise that you will raise it yourselves: you are never to tell your parents what happened this afternoon.' There was a chorus of 'Ohs!' but the man refused to listen. 'Either I have your promise or no chicken.'

It was a comfort to have the chicken, and it should have been nice eating the ices, for the man said they might as well, for it was simpler to return a pound than fourteen shillings, but worrying spoilt everything.

'If only it was a week day,' said Paul, 'we could get Mrs Gage to pawn something.'

Jane sighed. 'If it was a week day, darling Mrs Gage would lend it out of her Post Office savings.'

'Do you suppose Miss Bloggs . . .' Ginnie started to suggest, then she stopped, for Miss Bloggs was with their mother at the service in the Albert Hall.

Angus bounced with annoyance. 'It's preposterous,

we absolutely must know somebody rich who has a pound.'

But they did not know anybody rich, and feeling, as Jane said, wormish, they went home.

Mrs Gage saw at once something was wrong. She dug her fingers all over the chicken.

'It's not the fowl, for it's a lovely bird, Mr Gage wouldn't 'alf 'ave told off Ernie if it wasn't, so some-thin' else 'as 'appened. Cough it up! Troubles shared is troubles 'alved.' But when Mrs Gage heard what the trouble was she looked as gloomy as the children. 'This is a mess, this is. Mr Gage is out, or I'd get it off of 'im. I've only five shillings, did me weekend shoppin' last night. What time's 'e comin'?'

'He just said this evening,' Paul explained.

Mrs Gage whistled.

'Let's 'ope 'e comes early. Be a nice 'ow do you do if 'e comes when the MP's 'ere.' Then, because work helped her think, she began to clean the chicken, and suddenly she had an idea. 'We can't pay him, that's flat. You'll 'ave to give 'im an IOU, which is a lawful promise to pay tomorrow.'

'If you don't mind my saying so, Mrs Gage darling, that won't do,' said Ginnie. 'He said this evening, and he's a very mean-what-I-say sort of man.'

Mrs Gage put the chicken on a plate.

''e may be, but 'e 'asn't met me yet. 'e'll take the IOU. I've yet to meet the sauce-box who didn't take my say-so. Now, I don't want no more creatin'. 'ere's a bitta paper, write IOU on it, Paul, and you all put your names under. Then we'll 'ave our tea and forget our troubles till the front-door bell rings.'

But the front-door bell did not ring. It was five o'clock. It was six o'clock. It was seven o'clock and the man did not arrive.

'Oh, misery me,' Jane groaned, 'Daddy and Mummy will soon be back from evening church, and the visitor's coming at eight.'

Mrs Gage clicked her tongue against her teeth in a fussed way.

'While there's life there's 'ope, but you know what the Canon is, always one to jump up when the bell rings sayin' it's sure to be for 'im.'

Mrs Gage let them stay up as long as possible, but at last she had to send first Angus, and then Ginnie, up to bed.

'If you don't mind my saying so,' said Ginnie, 'Miss Virginia Bell calls this cruelty to children.'

'And a waste of time,' Angus pointed out. 'Me and Ginnie won't sleep till we know the man has his IOU.'

'I don't suppose they will,' Jane said. 'It will be all our shame if the Member of Parliament knows we had to borrow money to pay for his supper.'

It was a quarter to eight. It was ten to eight. It was five to eight. Then steps were heard outside. Mrs Gage stood in the kitchen door. Paul, holding the IOU, stood on the doormat, Jane hugged the end of the banisters, Ginnie and Angus, in their pyjamas, hung over the stairs. A key turned in the door.

'Hullo, Paul,' said Canon Bell, 'waiting for us? We've all arrived together.'

Cathy came in smiling, followed by the visitor.

'Come here, darlings. 'This is Mr Billet.'

There was a choking sound from Ginnie and Angus, who were halfway down the stairs, and a gasp from Jane. Mr Billet was the man in the check coat.

Paul kept his head, he gave his IOU to Mr Billet while shaking his hand.

Unnoticed by Canon and Mrs Bell, Mr Billet read the paper. Then he spoke in a loud voice, so that everybody could hear.

'Is there a fire about, old man? Would you burn this piece of paper? It's a private matter between myself and friends, and I never want to think about it again.'

Flag's Circus

Dan, Beth, Ruth and Tom were cousins, but they thought of themselves as brothers and sisters. Actually, unless they had been quads, they could not have been brothers and sisters, because they were all about the same age. All four were children of circus artistes, and had never known any other life than the circus world. Their grandfather, 'Ole-Man-Flag' as he became known in the profession, had inherited a small circus which possessed one sad old bear who danced, one mangy lion, a couple of wagons, a king pole, a very patched big top with tip-up seats, and a few dowdy props. Ole-Man-Flag, only he had been Young-Man-Flag in those days, had at first thought of selling his circus, but his wife, Rosie, had talked him out of it.

'I know we don't know much about circuses, ducks, but we can learn, can't we? And it's in your blood. You came into the circus through your Mum's folk.'

Circuses evidently were in Ole-Man-Flag's blood, for he very soon learned how to run his, and how to build up a good show. The first thing he did was to buy six matching grey horses, and a splendid Suffolk Punch for the bareback acts. He paid a Swedish artiste to run his horse acts and to teach his children what he knew, so it was not long before his five children were part of all the horse acts. All five rode in a bareback act called 'The Sharp-shooters'. The eldest girl, calling herself Mademoiselle Tina, wearing a ballet skirt and pink slippers, rode the rosin back, and skipped through paper hoops. The second boy, who had a real gift for handling horses, took over the training and exhibiting of the six grey liberties. It was that boy who, when he grew up, became Dan's father.

In time the old bear died, and so did the lion, and in their place Ole-Man-Flag bought a pair of clever chimpanzees and an elephant. There was no need to hire anyone to look after these, for the eldest girl, the

one who worked as Mademoiselle Tina, had been looking after the bear and the lion, so she took over both
the looking after and the training and exhibiting of
the newcomers. That girl, when she grew up, married a
flying-trapeze artiste. Their child was Beth.

The trapeze artiste, who was Beth's father, had a
sister who was also a flying-trapeze artiste; she married
another of the Flags, the youngest boy, who had a talent
for wire-walking, and was as well a good clown. Their
child was Ruth.

People belonging to a circus had to be able to turn
their hands to anything. The youngest of Ole-Man-Flag's
daughters, though she rode in the family bareback acts,
was not much use in the ring, but she was a wonderful
needlewoman. It was she who designed and made the
family's stage costumes, comic outfits for the clowns, and
even, on one occasion, when an accident had ruined his
proper one, a pink frock coat for Ole-Man-Flag to wear
as ringmaster. That daughter married a man who joined
the circus with a trampoline act. Their child was Tom.

With a background of circus as they had, it was no
wonder the Flag children had looked upon themselves
as circus artistes in the making ever since they had
understood anything. Each had learned to walk by
pushing a ball, nearly the size of themselves, round the

ring. Each had learned confidence by being tossed from one adult member of the family to another, with no more warning than 'look out, Tom', or Beth or whoever it was coming over. Sometimes on a Sunday, when of course there was no performance, the grown-up Flags would stand in the ring and play with the four babies as others would play with a ball. By the time the children could toddle all had little jobs round the circus. They helped feed the animals and to tidy the big top before performances. When they were a little older they sold tickets and programmes, and made themselves useful at the build-up and pull-down, the girls helping to pack and the boys to haul on guy ropes, to take their place in the line folding the canvas of the big top, and, when it rained, in spreading straw for the canvas to lie on. They all learned the sail-maker's craft of patching canvas, and they all helped groom the horses.

Behind the big top there was always a large mattress, and on this the four children were taught to tumble. They learned a regular routine and had to practise it for half an hour each day until they became so good at flip-flaps, backward somersaults and cartwheels they were supple all over, and could fall off anything without being hurt, which is the beginning of all circus training. In the ring they were taught to ride by Dan's father. At first they wore a lunge, but soon they were riding bareback and jumping on and off the rosin back, and that often meant falls. Beth's father gave them lessons on his flying trapeze. Of course there was a net, but they were in it often and they might have been badly hurt if they had not first learned to tumble. Ruth's father taught them to walk on a wire. He started them off when they were tiny on a rope stretched six inches above a mattress, but soon they were working on the proper wire in the ring, and that meant a lot of tumbles too. Tom's father taught them to work on the trampoline, and that was where their tumbling was used as tumbling, for on the trampoline they could do their whole routine.

Of course the children had to go to school. Mostly Flag's Circus did three-day stands, but sometimes it was just one day. But whether it was one day or three, Ole-Man-Flag packed his grandchildren off to school, for that was the law, and he was fussy about keeping the law. The children did not find it odd going to different schools every few days because they were used to it, but they none of them cared for lessons, and so never learned much, and that was how trouble came to them.

The eldest son of Ole-Man-Flag, whose name was Duke, had left the circus. Although of course, like the rest of his family, he had been brought up to it, he had never thought it respectable, and as soon as he could he gave it up and went into the grocery business. The children had heard of their Uncle Duke, but had never seen him. He was a sort of fairy-tale figure. 'As rich as Duke' was a saying with the Flags, and so was 'As lady-like as Lily'; Lily was Duke's wife. But one year the circus booked a three-night stand in a little place in northern England, which was where Duke lived.

'Bloodstock and Brimstone,' said Ole-Man-Flag when he fixed the date. 'Close to where Duke lives! Won't half be a treat to see his dial again.'

Duke Flag, Mrs Duke Flag and the three Flag children, Geraldine, Fitzroy and Felix, were very, very grand and very, very proper, and so were not at all pleased when their circus relations, of whom they were ashamed, settled down in a field near them. They were shocked to find every wall carrying a poster saying 'Flag's Circus'. Although Duke Flag had made his money in a chain of grocery stores there was not one in the refined neighbourhood in which he lived, so he was just accepted as a pillar of society. He lived in a pillar-of-society house, which was modern Tudor, with a hint of Norman castle.

'Very bad taste of them to come here,' Duke said to Lily. 'I suppose we must do what we can to be pleasant, but we mustn't go too far.'

Doing what they could to be pleasant meant visiting the circus once, and asking all the circus Flags to tea on Sunday.

The adult circus Flags could not imagine anyone would look down on them. They supposed they lived a glorious life; before they visited Duke's home they could not imagine a better. They looked forward to Sunday as a proper treat, and supposed Duke was feeling the same. What could be nicer than a family reunion?

The circus Flags had not been long in Duke's home before his way of life, and the way he talked, began to make them feel inferior. His house was so important-looking. The carpets so thick and so soft. His furniture so shiny and so beautifully upholstered. They were used to shouting to each other, but in Duke's house they almost spoke in whispers, because clearly a raised voice was bad manners. But it was when they came to talk of their children that the circus Flags began to feel low as worms.

'There's nothing to touch a good schooling,' said Duke. 'I know you did your best, Father, but of course we can all see now what we missed. Geraldine, Fitzroy and Felix are having a real slap-up education at the best boarding schools money can buy. No expense spared, is my motto, when it comes to education.'

Ole-Man-Flag, though he felt a bit humble inside, managed to assert himself.

'Brimstone and treacle, you've not done so bad, Duke old boy, with the education I gave you.'

Duke looked proud.

'Self-made and not ashamed of it; but what I say is, because you've been through the mill no reason why your children should do the same. Proper little lady and gents they'll be, fit to take their place with the highest in the land.'

Perhaps Duke's talk about education would not have had so much effect if at that moment Geraldine, Fitzroy and Felix had not come into the room with Dan, Beth, Ruth and Tom. Geraldine, Fitzroy and Felix were the sort of children who looked as if they brushed their hair, cleaned their teeth and washed, not by order, but for pleasure. Back in the circus Dan, Beth, Ruth and Tom looked all right. Before they had started out they had of course washed and brushed their hair, but somehow, against Geraldine, Fitzroy and Felix, they looked as though they had never used a comb, and had scarcely heard of toothbrushes or soap. But it was when Duke ordered his children to display the good education they were having that the circus Flags realised that by Duke's standards their children were shabby ignoramuses.

'Fitzroy,' said Duke, 'if two trains are travelling, one from Edinburgh and the other from London, the Edinburgh train at a speed of 76 miles an hour, the London train at 82 miles an hour, how far will each be from its destination when they pass each other?'

The circus Flags knew, even before he spoke, that Fitzroy would know the answer and very depressed it made them, for Fitzroy was almost twelve, which was the same age as Dan, Beth, Ruth and Tom, who could barely do simple addition. Duke raised a finger, and pointed to Geraldine.

'Let's hear how nicely you speak French.'

Geraldine stood up.

'*Maître Corbeau sur un arbre perché* ...'

To the circus Flags Geraldine's performance was miraculous. From time to time they had known French circus artistes, and out of sheer politeness had now and again replied to their broken English 'Wee, wee', or 'Nong, nong'. But that was as far as their French went.

Duke then beckoned to Felix, who was only eight.

'Who was the father of William the Conqueror?'

Felix, looking smug, answered immediately.

'Robert the Magnificent, 1028 to 1035.'

Duke, with a gesture to show that no knowledge was

hidden from Felix, invited the circus Flags to question him, but the circus Flags refused. Each was painfully aware that they did not know a suitable question to ask a boy who knew not only the name, but the dates of William the Conqueror's father.

After tea Duke took his father and brothers out to see his garden, and it was then that Ole-Man-Flag put out a feeler.

'Cauliflower and teapots, I suppose it would be a bit late to send our four to boarding schools?'

Duke considered the question.

'In the ordinary way I would say yes, but with my influence something might be done. Her school is very proud of my Geraldine, so maybe they would find room for Beth and Ruth. If Dan and Tom appreciate how hard they'll have to work to catch up I'll have a word with the headmaster of Fitzroy and Felix's school.'

The awful news of what was planned for them did not reach Dan, Beth, Ruth and Tom until two weeks later. By that time everything was arranged. Duke had used his influence. The headmistress of Geraldine's school was prepared, as a favour, to take Beth and Ruth. The headmaster of Fitzroy and Felix's school would take Dan and Tom for a term on trial. The four children said very little when the news was broken to them, but at once ran to their parliament place, which was the mattress on which they had learned to tumble.

'Imagine,' said Beth, 'to go to school with that awful Geraldine.'

'Learning to recite in French,' Ruth moaned.

'Looking all prunish and primish,' said Beth.

Tom stood on his hands.

'Thank goodness Dan and I are only going for a term on trial. I bet they won't have us at the end of that.'

Dan was turning one cartwheel after another, they always helped him to think. He finished with a flip-flap.

'Don't let's go.'

The other three looked at him amazed.

'But we are going,' said Beth.

'It's all fixed,' Tom pointed out.

Dan squatted down on the mattress. With a gesture he made the other three lean forward.

'I'm sure it can be un-fixed, and I think I know a way.'

'How?' asked Beth.

Dan chewed a piece of grass.

'We've got to show them they can't run Flag's without us.'

'But they can,' Tom argued. 'I know we're useful and all that, but they won't have to hire anyone extra in our place. The family will just work extra hard, and do the things we do now. After all, it isn't as if we were old enough to perform in the ring.'

'But we are!' said Ruth. 'I mean, we will be next week. You can have a performer's licence when you're twelve.'

Beth hugged her knees to her.

'What could we do? I mean, we can all ride in the bareback acts, but it goes over all right without us.'

'And I suppose soon we could manage the flying trapeze, and the high wire, but they're doing all right too.'

It was Dan who had the idea.

'I know! A funny act! Grandfather always says we're low on comedy stuff. There's another five weeks before those awful schools start, and with any luck somebody will get ill, or something, before then, and we'll step in and say we've an act we can do. I bet Grandfather won't let us go after that.'

Getting an act ready without any of the grown-ups knowing was very difficult. It meant rehearsing away from the circus ground, and it meant using up every second of their free time. But all four children were ambitious and hard-working. At the end of two and a half weeks an act had taken shape. Ruth, who was much the smallest of the four, was to come into the ring dressed as a fox. She was to give a short display of tumbling, then on would come Beth and Tom, dressed as hounds. For this they had worked out a kind of funny obstacle race. They had a piece of tubing through which they wriggled, a fence over which they climbed, and, of course, there was a lot of funny business on the ring fence. There was a comedy pool of water, across which all three pretended to swim, and a comedy tree, up which Ruth climbed, which then swayed to and fro, first to Beth and then to Tom.

While the hunt was still in progress Dan, in a funny sporting outfit, was to come on with an enormous water pistol, and pail of water. The act was to finish with the fox, hounds and the sportsman being drenched to the skin.

All the children were good with their fingers. With their savings they bought artificial fur fabric, which the girls turned into dogs' and fox skins. Out of some old props they built a comedy sporting outfit for Dan. Meanwhile Dan and Tom made a fence, a tree and a comedy pond. In a circus everything, when packed, has its proper place, and it is very difficult to hide anything, but there was one wagon which was more or less in the boys' charge, so in the back of it they hide their props and clothes.

Two weeks went by, and no act was off or even late. The children were nearly desperate. Two weeks before school term! Something must happen now, or it would be too late.

The night before the children were to go to their boarding schools, the circus was playing in north Wales. Though it was their last night, the children were busy with their usual jobs: they acted as grooms, they sold programmes, they showed the people into their seats. The performance started normally with the parade, then Dan's father rode as the Moscow Courier; that was followed by Beth's mother and her chimpanzees, and that by Ruth's parents in their flying-trapeze act. This should have been followed by Dan's father and the grey liberties, but instead, while Ruth's parents were still in the air, Dan's father came into the ring and whispered to Ole-Man-Flag. The old man appeared unmoved, but after Ruth's parents had bowed themselves out, instead of number four flashing on the programme board, he came to the centre of the ring.

'Melords, Ladies and Gentlemen. There will be a small interval before Monsieur Popopski' (that was what Dan's father called himself) 'shows his equine marvels, the six liberty greys. During the wait the band will play a march by Sousa.'

The band was Grandmother, putting records on the gramophone, which was relayed to the audience by loud-speaker. The children were standing in the entrance. Ole-Man-Flag went across to them.

'There's a fire in the horse tent. Everybody's there putting it out. Could you kids do something? Don't want the audience smelling smoke and panicking.'

The wagon in which the clothes and props were hidden was close to the big top. It was only a matter of minutes to drag everything out, and dress themselves. It was a matter of seconds to give Grandfather the props and tell him where they should be set up. Then Dan gave Ruth a push.

'On you go. Good luck to us all.'

Grandmother was clever with records, she could lay her hand on any record at a moment's notice. Peering into the ring she saw Ruth's entrance and at once recognised that she was a fox. In a moment Sousa was switched off and 'A-hunting we will go' was switched on.

There is nothing more popular with an audience than an unexpected turn, and nothing goes down better than performances by children. To the audience Ruth did not look more than eight, so amazed gasps followed the little fox through her spins and cartwheels. When the hounds came on the gasps turned to laughter, and when the sportsman appeared the laughter became roars. If there is one thing that every circus audience is sure to enjoy it is seeing people get wet. Dan, born and bred in a circus, had thought of that, and his Grandfather, watching the act, thought of that too. Every time Dan's bucket was empty he threw it to Grandfather, who quickly refilled it. There never were four wetter people than Dan, Beth, Ruth and Tom. During the act a little smoke blew across the big top, but nobody noticed it, and before the last bucket of water was thrown the fire was out. Four times the children had to come back and bow before the audience would let them go.

That night, after the pull-down, there was a little celebration in and outside Ole-Man-Flag's caravan. Ole-Man-Flag made a speech.

'Family and members of my circus. Cheese and potatoes, this has been quite a night! I have to thank you one and all for the prompt way you put out the fire in the horse lines. It was very smartly done, no panic, and not a hair of a horse's tail singed. Though, mind you, if a hair had been singed I'd have taken a horsewhip to you grooms.' There was laughter there, for everyone knew Ole-Man-Flag's bark was worse than his bite. 'While you were putting out the fire something very surprising was happening in the ring. Come here, children.' Dan, Beth, Ruth and Tom stood in front of Grandfather. 'You don't want to go to those schools tomorrow, do you?' The children shook their heads violently. 'I thought as much. So you worked up this act to show me I couldn't do without you, didn't you?' The children nodded again. 'And I suppose you think I'm going to say from now on you can work in the ring.'

The children felt awful. Dan whispered:

'Yes, sir.'

Grandfather waited a moment before he went on. 'Port and radishes, your Uncle Duke was right when he said schooling was important. Suppose, mind you I only said suppose, I was to let you work in my circus, could I have your promise that from this time on you'll all attend to your books?'

Tom looked at Ruth, Ruth looked at Beth, they all looked at Dan. Their eyes told him to answer for them.

'We promise, Grandfather. If you let us stay and work for you we'll slave at school, honestly we will. We'll even do homework.'

Grandfather looked pleased.

'Tomatoes and sausages, that's fine! But mind, if you break your word you go to those boarding schools, that's flat. Now off to bed with you. We've an early start tomorrow.'

Everybody drifted back to their caravans. Ole-Man-Flag was alone with his Rosie. Presently he began to chuckle.

'Popcorn and marmalade! Course Duke's right, there's nothing like good schooling, but between ourselves, Rosie, I'd rather have our four than his Geraldine, Fitzroy and Felix. What do you say?'

Rosie smiled.

'Too right, ducks. Now do come to bed, or we'll never start in the morning.'

The Secret

It was a spring morning just before the end of term. Janet Jameson walked slowly up the steps to the pupils' entrance of the Allison School for Stage Training. Janet's shoulders were sagging, in fact she drooped all over with depression. 'How awful,' she thought. 'Here is Janet Jameson coming up the pupils' steps for the last time. I shall never again feel the gorgeousness of being at a proper training school. I will just go back to the ordinary world outside.' She opened the door. She stood on the mat and sniffed; classes were held in the art of make-up, so there was a faint smell of greasepaint and powder in the air. To Janet it was the most perfect smell in the world. She gulped back a sob and walked slowly down the stairs to the changing-room. 'This is the last time. I must remember every foot of this. The jagged bit sticking out from this step. The shiny piece of carpet at the bottom because we all jump the last three steps. The letter B on the changing-room door. The feel of the door handle in my hand. The voices that rush to meet me as I open the door.'

Outside the changing-room door Janet paused to straighten her shoulders. She was not pretty, but she had an unusual, attractive face. Pale and thin, with large grey-green eyes. Her heavy dark hair, which fell into the nape of her neck, suited her perfectly. Just at the moment her face lacked animation, but at other times, when she was happy and interested, she had a vividness of expression that was quite outstanding.

Fourteen girls shared B dressing-room. They were in various stages of changing. Few of the Allison girls had much money to spare, so there were no regulations about uniform. For the acting classes they wore anything they liked and when, as now, they changed for dancing, they put on something which gave free movement and allowed the teacher to see what their legs were up to. Janet had a skimpy silk tunic she had made out of a worn-out summer frock. She opened her locker and took it off its hanger. From the back of the locker she pulled out her pink ballet shoes. Janet's ambition was to be a straight actress, but the sight of her ballet shoes brought a new lump into her throat. She enjoyed dancing and she knew it was good training for an actress. She would never forget the thrill the day she was promoted to block shoes. When would she wear them again? Never, most likely.

'What's up? You do look miserable.'

Janet swallowed the lump and smiled. It was difficult to be gloomy with Sally about. Sally was in the school's opinion the star pupil, for she not only showed promise as an actress, but she could sing, and was not a bad dancer. As well she was lovely to look at. Flaming copper-coloured hair. Huge blue eyes with black lashes. The perfect complexion that sometimes goes with red hair. Janet sat on the floor to put on her ballet shoes.

'I'm feeling end-of-termish.'

Sally was quick at feeling things about anybody, and particularly about people she was fond of. She was very fond of Janet. She put an arm round her shoulders.

'What's up?'

Janet was afraid she was going to cry. She whispered in a fierce sort of way.

'Can't explain.' To prevent any further questioning she got up and began dragging her frock over her head.

Sally, too, got up. She glanced round to see if the other girls were listening. Nobody but herself had noticed that anything was wrong with Janet. Most of the girls had changed and were filling the time before their class limbering up. Sally pulled Janet out of her frock and hung it up for her.

'I won't ask you just now, but you've simply got to tell me what's wrong.'

The ballet classes were held in the main hall. Down each side were practice barres. At the end was a small stage on which was a piano. Sergius, who taught the school, had not yet arrived, so the girls limbered up.

Janet was next to a girl called Celia, who was trying for a place in a ballet on television.

'Oh goodness,' Celia said, 'I'm sure Sergius will think I haven't practised, but I have, but it's so difficult at home, the people underneath make an awful row if I bump.'

There was a murmur of sympathy. Most of the class lived in flats and knew from bitter experience what the people underneath thought about dancing practice. Janet raised herself on her pointes.

'Thank goodness it's you that's going to the audition, not me.'

Celia set her feet wide apart in the first position, and bent her knees.

'You can thank your stars you want to be an actress; underneath flats, however nasty the people in them, can't mind a person practising to be an actress over their heads.'

Sally, who was in the middle of a plié, straightened up.

'That's all you know. I was rehearsing Katherine in a scene with Petruchio, and the man below us beat on the door and said if I couldn't argue more quietly he'd call the police.'

Janet's eyes seemed to have a lamp in them.

'I wouldn't care how much anybody beat on the door or what anybody said, if I wanted to work at a part I'd work anywhere, in the road, in a train, even in the middle of Piccadilly Circus.'

The other girls gathered round. One of them said:

'Janet's off again, we know where you got that from.'

All the class looked up at the wall above Janet's head. Round the hall photographs of great actors and actresses of the past and the present. One family was especially represented, the Billingtons. There had been

Billington stars for four generations. Over Janet's head was a photograph of a young girl in the part of Nell Gwyn.

Sally looked up at the photograph.

'Judy Billington. She must have been simply gorgeous. I wish, oh, how I wish I'd seen her.'

Celia changed the position of her feet and once more bent her knees.

'Mrs Allison says she forgot everything when she thought about a part. Once she saw her being Nell Gwyn on Holborn Underground Station. Such a place to choose!'

Janet spoke quickly.

'She wasn't showing off, she just thought of something for the part, and then, of course, she had to try it out, she just forgot where she was.'

Celia laughed.

'To hear you one would think you'd seen her if one didn't know she had stopped acting before you were born.'

Sally lifted her left leg over her head.

'There's no harm in anyone having an idol, and we all know Judy Billington is Janet's.' She stood on her pointes staring at the photograph. 'She must have been terribly in love. Of course I haven't been in love yet, but if I was I'm quite sure I wouldn't give up my career to be married. I bet she's sorry now that she did.'

Janet gazed up at the picture.

'I'm sure she's sorry sometimes, but the man she married hates the theatre, so she promised to give it up, and she's stuck to it. I do hope if I'm ever an actress I won't fall in love, or if I do it will be with someone who loves the theatre.'

Sally nudged Janet.

'Ssh! Sergius.'

Half an hour later Sergius signed to the pianist to stop playing.

'Rest, young ladies.' The fourteen girls thankfully relaxed. They leaned against the practice barres and moved their toes up and down in their shoes to ease their insteps. Sergius nodded to the pianist. 'We will now take the leetle variations.' He turned to Celia. 'Mees Celia,' he waved a hand. 'Young ladies, you may sit.'

The girls ran to a bench at the bottom of the room. They picked up their cardigans as they ran and either put them on or hung them round their shoulders. Sally put her arm through Janet's.

'Come on. Right up in that corner and then the others won't hear.'

Janet had not meant to tell anybody about herself, but

it was difficult to keep Sally at arm's length. Besides, it would be nice to confide in somebody. Not everything, of course; she could never tell anybody everything. The big secret she must keep to herself, but she could explain about it being her last term. That would be a help; it was so hateful being miserable alone.

'I'm not coming back next term.'

Sally was so surprised that she felt as if the wind had been knocked out of her.

'Not coming back! Why on earth not? You are doing so well at the acting classes. You aren't fourteen yet. You've years of training to do.'

'It's the money. There isn't any more.'

Sally was puzzled, and not for the first time. Janet was not poor, in fact her clothes were better than most of the girls' in the school. There was obviously something queer about Janet's home, for she hated talking about it. But this time Sally decided she must be made to.

'Has your father lost his job?'

Janet fidgeted with the hem of her tunic.

'No. You won't understand, Sally, because I can't explain about me. There's a good reason – my father and mother don't know I'm training here. As a matter of fact, I pay for myself.'

'Pay for yourself! Your family don't know?' Suddenly

the corners of Sally's eyes crinkled and she began to laugh. 'You, of all people, looking so quiet and so yes-sir-no-sir-three-bags-fullish. How do you manage to fool them?'

Janet flushed.

'I haven't fooled them exactly. I'd hate to do it. I was desperate to think I was growing up without any proper stage training. The school I go to doesn't work on Saturdays, so Saturday mornings are all right. When I come here on Mondays, Wednesdays and Fridays I'm supposed to be at my piano lessons.'

Sally giggled.

'What happens about those? I should like to be around when your family ask you to play the "Moonlight Sonata" and you can't strike a note.'

'Oh, but I can play.' Janet hesitated, choosing her words carefully. 'The person who teaches me is a revelation; he knows why I have to wangle to come here. He gives me a quick music lesson before school twice a week, and two hours on Saturday afternoons.'

'Gosh! Every Saturday? How simply awful. I couldn't give up every Saturday afternoon. I'd never get to a matinée.'

Janet lifted one leg on to the bench and hugged it to her.

'No, it is awful, but I want so terribly to be a good actress, I simply had to have some coaching. I've known about the Allison school ever since I was born. Mrs Allison's got an international reputation as a teacher, you know. I simply had to learn from her.'

Sally continued to probe.

'If your family don't know, how did you get the money to come here?'

'Presents. It was in the Post Office.'

Sally let out a big breath.

'Janet Jameson, you surprise me more every minute. Do you mean to say you drew all your money out of the Post Office without asking your dad if you might? And having got it out you blew the whole lot on coming here?'

'Yes.'

'And now you've nothing in the Post Office?'

'Only five shillings. I left that so that I could keep my book.'

Sally was really distressed.

'But, after spending all that money, you can't leave now, you're so awfully promising, you were perfect in that scene from *St Joan* last term.'

Janet let both her legs sprawl in front of her in a hopeless sort of way.

'I've thought of everything, even selling something, but the only jewellery I've got my mother looks after.'

Sally swung round on the bench. She spoke in a whisper.

'If I tell you something will you absolutely swear not to tell the others?'

'Of course.'

'Well, I may be going to play in a revival. It's Margaret in *Dear Brutus*. The Glay Management may put it on.'

'Margaret!'

Sally nodded.

'Mrs Allison said to say nothing until we're sure because it's unlucky.'

Janet gasped.

'Margaret! How gorgeous for you.'

Sally brushed aside Janet's interruption.

'I have an idea that might help you. If the Glay Management do revive *Dear Brutus* I don't suppose they've got an understudy. They were only going to make up their minds this weekend, so they won't have got far about engaging understudies. Why don't you go to Mrs Allison? Tell her what you've just told me. You can explain that I told you about *Dear Brutus* and ask her if she would recommend you for the understudy. She thinks an awful lot of your work; you know she does.'

Janet stared at Sally, her eyes bigger than usual with excitement.

'What a marvellous idea,' she thought. If only it could come true. It would not only be the money, it would mean being in a theatre. Acting on a real stage at understudy rehearsals. Enough money for the fees for next term. Perhaps, if the revival ran long enough, for lots of terms. She jumped to her feet and caught hold of Sally's arm.

'Come with me after class and talk to Mrs Allison.'

Sergius was calling. 'Come, young ladies. Come to the centre.'

Sally nodded. 'All right, directly after class is over, just as soon as we have changed.'

Mrs Allison was at her office desk when Sally tapped on her door. She smiled at the two girls.

'Well?'

Sally was shy of nobody. She drew a chair up by the desk and in a minute was pouring out Janet's troubles. Mrs Allison held out a hand to Janet who was standing awkwardly, listening.

'I think you might have told me all this before.'

Janet looked at the carpet and rubbed it up the wrong way with the toe of her ballet shoe.

'There are reasons.'

Mrs Allison turned over her ledger.

'Your fees are paid by a Mr Jameson. Who's he?'

Janet was crimson.

'He teaches me the piano.'

'A relation?'

'Yes. My brother.'

Mrs Allison tapped her ledger with a pencil.

'A parent has to sign a contract, you know, if you were engaged.'

Janet swallowed nervously.

'I sometimes think my mother guesses.'

Mrs Allison leaned forward to say something more, but before she could speak her secretary knocked and came in. The secretary was a flustered little woman and now she looked scared.

'It's Mr Glay.'

Mrs Allison was quite unmoved.

'Ask him to come in.' Sally's hand was lying on her desk. She patted it. 'Now we shall know your fate.' Janet was turning to leave the room; she stopped her. 'No, stay. We'll see what we can do about this under-study.'

Mr Glay began to speak almost before he was in the room.

'This is a wonderful opportunity for you, young lady, a wonderful opportunity. Margaret is a peach of a part. One of the most moving scenes in any play.'

Mrs Allison held out her hand and drew Sally to her.

'Congratulations, my child. Now Mr Glay and I have got to talk business. You run along home and tell your parents. I knows they'll be proud.' She waited until the door was shut, then she turned to Mr Glay. 'Do you want an understudy for Margaret?'

Mr Glay nodded.

'I haven't engaged one yet.'

Mrs Allison smiled at Janet.

'Then may I recommend this child? Her name is Janet Jameson.'

Mr Glay studied Janet. She was not his idea of the part, for he wanted a strikingly pretty child, with curls. Still, there was no reason why Sally should ever be off. It was not a bad idea, having another girl from the same school. He settled himself in a chair and turned to Janet.

'Let's hear you recite something.'

Janet moved to the middle of the room. She closed her eyes for a moment to get rid of Mrs Allison and Mr

Glay, and to feel away by herself. Mrs Allison watched her with a half-smile. She glanced at Mr Glay to see if he saw what she saw, but Mr Glay was looking at the ceiling.

Janet had left Mrs Allison's room. She was St Joan speaking to her jailers. Centuries fell away, she grew older and taller, her voice took on a country burr.

When she finished her speech there was for a moment complete silence, before Mr Glay turned to Mrs Allison.

'She'll do.'

The rehearsals for *Dear Brutus* went fairly well, but Sally found that playing a part at a stage school and playing a part in a real production were two very different things. Every line, and every inflection was important, every bit of business and step taken had to be marked in the prompt book. *Dear Brutus* was a play which had been first acted early in the nineteen-twenties. It had been acted very often since and, as happens when plays are revived, moves and inflections put in by previous actors had become part of the production, and it was difficult to get away from them. In the play the part of Margaret was a dream daughter of an artist called Dearth. He had never had a daughter and his dream child was the daughter he ought to have had. Sir J. M. Barrie, in the stage directions, said of Margaret: 'She is as lovely as you think she is, and she is aged the moment when you like your daughter best.'

The man who was playing Dearth in the Glay Management's revival, Basil Kingston, was a very distinguished actor indeed. It had been his idea that a real child ought to play Margaret, and that she ought not to look more than twelve or thirteen. In previous productions a grown-up actress had played Margaret, and she had looked as if she was fifteen or sixteen. The actor who played Dearth knew exactly what he wanted Margaret to be like. Rather hoydenish, very unsophisticated, and with absolute understanding between herself and her father. Sally was Mr Glay's choice; to Basil Kingston she was too pretty-pretty and though he thought she was clever he was not entirely pleased with her acting. He kept saying to her: 'Don't do so much. Just be a simple little girl.'

Sometimes Sally would lose her temper with him and say: 'How can I be simple when everything I do is fixed and arranged and I can't make one spontaneous movement?'

After rehearsals Basil Kingston would talk to Sally exactly as if she were his daughter. He would ask her how much pocket money she had, and if she was getting short to tell him, and he would give her the sort of presents a father would give a daughter, and he teased her. He liked Sally, but treating her as his daughter was for the good of the play. He knew that if Sally could feel easy with him and he with her they would act much better together.

In the half-dark theatre Janet sat with the understudies, marking in her copy every direction given to Sally. Cross left. Stand on one leg. Lean against the tree and while you speak play with the bark. As well, she listened to all Basil Kingston said, and stored it away in her mind.

Directly Sally's rehearsal was over, and except for a little entrance at the end she was only concerned with one act, she and Janet joined the teacher from the school who was chaperoning them, and discussed how things had gone.

'They aren't pleased with me. Mr Kingston isn't pleased, I can feel he isn't,' Sally would moan. Or, on days when things went better: 'It was a gorgeous rehearsal today.'

Janet let Sally think that she agreed with her when

she was pleased, and disagreed with her when she was depressed, for it was no good fussing Sally, who was sufficiently worked up already. But loyal as Janet was to Sally she did not always agree with the way she played Margaret, and she knew the other understudies did not either. Particularly she disagreed with the way Sally said the lines that brought down the curtain. Dearth and his daughter had been having a lovely time in the wood, Dearth painting and Margaret talking, as a daughter would to her father, about what she was going to be like when she was grown up, and about what she was like when she was little. Then they began talking about losing each other, and from that moment the wood began to fade. The father became more real and Margaret more of a dream. Just as the curtain fell Margaret grew frightened and tried to call her father back. She ran from tree to tree, and the stage directions said: 'We begin to lose her among the shadows'. Then Margaret had to call out: 'Daddy, come back; I don't want to be a might-have-been.' To Janet this moment was for Margaret unbearable; how terrible to be only a dream, to see your father walk towards a real house and real people and know that you only lived in his imagination.

Sally felt the end differently. She thought Margaret

said: 'I don't want to be a might-have-been' because she knew that she was interesting and vital, so it was wrong that she should remain a dream and never come alive. She did not feel, as Janet did, the appalling horror of the darkening wood and the child lost and forgotten.

A week before the production day Sally arrived at rehearsal looking ill. The teacher from the school said:

'You do look white, child; what's the matter?'

Sally answered rudely.

'Nothing. What should there be?' To Janet she told the truth. 'I can't think what's up. I keep getting an awful pain and I was sick three times in the night.'

'Does your mother know?'

'Of course not. She wouldn't have let me get up. Oh, Janet, I can't be going to be ill. My lovely, lovely part!'

The rehearsal went badly, for Sally was slow and stupid. Basil Kingston would not scold her because he thought she might get frightened of him, and so they would lose their easy father-and-daughter atmosphere on the stage, but Janet could see he was exasperated inside.

Margaret's first entrance was to race her father on

to the stage. They were looking for the place where Dearth had put his painting easel the night before. Margaret's first line was: 'Daddy, Daddy, I have won. Here is the place. Crack-in-my-eye Tommy!' 'Crack-in-my-eye Tommy' was Margaret's nickname for her father. The whole line needed saying with great gaiety but complete naturalness. As a rule Sally was charming in that entrance, but today she simply could not do it; she sounded lifeless and, because she was trying to put in life where she did not feel it, affected. After three attempts at the line Basil Kingston let it pass and they went on with the scene, but it was a sad, grey performance, and then they came to the bit where Margaret pretended to be grown up and put up her hair. She had to kneel by a pool and say:

MARGARET: [*on her knees among the leaves*] Daddy, now I'm putting up my hair. I have got such a darling of a mirror. It is such a darling mirror I've got, Dad. Dad, don't look. I shall tell you about it. It is a little pool of water. I wish we could take it home and hang it up. Of course the moment my hair is up there will be other changes also; for instance, I shall talk quite differently.

While Sally was saying this speech she had to pull her curls to the top of her head and fasten them up there with a little piece of bracken. When she got up from the pool she was supposed to look something like what the grown-up Margaret might have looked. That morning, as she fumbled with her curls, her voice seemed to tail away, and when she tried to get up she succeeded only in raising her head, and her face was green. She opened her mouth to say her next lines, but before a sound came out she crumpled up on the floor.

Sally was carried to her dressing-room and the faint seemed nothing at first, but when she recovered from it she still seemed so ill a doctor was sent for. A few minutes after he arrived the bad news was all over the theatre. Sally had an inflamed appendix. She was to be operated on immediately.

Janet, sitting in the stalls clutching her script, felt her inside turning over and over. 'How awful. Poor Sally!' Then she thought of herself. 'Oh goodness, I shall have to play at this rehearsal.' She shut her eyes and whispered: 'Let me act well. Let me act really well.'

The stage manager, Basil Kingston and Mr Glay were having a conversation on the stage. Suddenly the stage manager came to the footlights. With one hand he shaded his eyes from the glare and peered into the stalls.

'Is Janet Jameson there? Come up here, my dear, we want you.'

Janet hardly heard the muttered 'Good luck, Janet' of the other understudies. Her heart was beating too fast; she stumbled out of her seat and through the pass door on to the stage.

The principals had not seen Janet before; they looked at her with interest and kind smiles. She tried to smile back but her mouth felt stiff. The wood scene was up that morning. Queer, thin trees, which under the proper lighting would have the enchantment of moonlight. The wood had appeared magically at the end of act one. When the act started there had been a garden outside the window, but when it finished there was a wood of trees pressed close to the pane. Everybody in the play, except the child Margaret, was a guest in the house of a queer old man called Lob, and each of the guests thought they could have been much happier if they had a second chance in life. In act two, in the wood, they got the second chance that they wanted and, of course, found out that human nature doesn't change even with second chances.

Because of Sally's illness and the upset it had caused, Basil Kingston had decided they would take act two all over again. Margaret did not come on until halfway through the act. The other characters, wandering about two-and-two, were in the wood first. Janet stood in the wings; she knew her cue, and she knew her lines, but could she make her voice speak? She was panting as if she had been running. Take deep breaths when you're nervous, Mrs Allison had taught her. She took a deep breath, and then another. Then she felt a hand on her shoulder. Basil Kingston smiled down at her. He did not seem to notice that she was nervous. He did not even seem to know that he had never spoken to her before.

'A nice night for a stroll in the woods, daughter, but you ought to be in bed, you know.'

Janet found it difficult even to whisper:

'I suppose it is late as the moon's out.'

He rearranged her hair on her shoulders.

'Silly daughter. Of course it's late, you've not been out at this time since we went bathing by moonlight.'

Suddenly Janet stopped being frightened and entered into the spirit of the game. If he was her pretence father, she could make up stories for a pretence daughter.

'And then we sat on the beach and ate strawberries and cream.'

He laughed.

'Highly indigestible at that time of night, especially

when accompanied by lobster. It was lobster we ate, wasn't it?'

Janet nodded.

'And then we had ice cream.'

He gave her shoulder an affectionate pat.

'Off we go then. The nightingale is singing and the wood is all ours. Which of us is going to find my painting easel first?'

It was almost easy after that. When you had played at being father and daughter off-stage it was only natural to go on being father and daughter on the stage. After a very few minutes Janet was enjoying herself. It was such sensible conversation that she and Mr Kingston had to have. Just like the conversation they had both been making up.

MARGARET: The moon is rather pale tonight,
 isn't she?
DEARTH: Comes of keeping late hours.
MARGARET: [*showing off*] Daddy, watch me, look at
 me. Please, sweet moon, a pleasant expression.
 No, no, not as if you were sitting for it; that
 is too professional. That is better; thank you.
 Now keep it. That is the sort of thing you say to
 them, Dad.

DEARTH: I oughtn't to have brought you out so
  late; you should be tucked up in your cosy bed at
  home.

It was not difficult to feel the end of the play, for
Janet was no longer Janet. She was Margaret, and when
she saw Mr Kingston walking off towards Lob's lighted
house, a sort of panic came over her. Once inside there,
with all the other real people, he would forget that alone
in the middle of a darkening wood was a daughter who
was only a dream. Terrified, she ran from tree to tree;
her voice rang through the theatre.

'Daddy, come back; I don't want to be a might-have-
been.'

Mr Glay, Mr Kingston and, surprisingly, Mrs Allison,
whom Janet had not supposed was in the theatre, were
whispering on the stage. Janet stood watching them
with a queer feeling of slowly coming out of being
Margaret and back into being Janet. Then Mr Glay
beckoned to her, he held out his hand and drew her
into the group.

'We're very pleased with you, young lady. If you work

hard in the next few days you should give a very touching performance.'

Mrs Allison stooped and kissed Janet.

'Well done, my child. This is a wonderful chance for you.'

Basil Kingston put his arm round her. He raised her chin.

'I'm looking forward to knowing more of my new daughter, but somewhere I feel as if we had met before.'

It was the first night. Janet's dresser gave the green skirt Janet was wearing a last tweak. The teacher from the school and the girl who had become Janet's understudy wished her luck. Janet took a quick look at herself in the glass: she looked very ordinary, she thought, in a jersey and skirt with bare legs and sandals, but she was improved by a little make-up. It was a pity she had not Sally's red hair, Sally looked glorious in green. There was a knock on her dressing-room door; it was the call boy.

'Miss Jameson, your entrance, please.'

Janet took a deep breath and, followed by the teacher, went up on to the side of the stage, passing the canvas scenery backs, and mysterious silver-blue lighting from arcs and battens; she could hear the voices of 'Mabel' and 'Purdie', two characters in the scene before her entrance. Stepping quietly, she moved into the wings.

It was lovely to find Mr Kingston waiting. He had got over his nerves in the first act so he was quite unflustered.

'My word! The wood looks nice. Doesn't the bracken smell good?'

Janet peered on to the stage. It was bathed in moonlight and the trees were queer and ghostly. There was no bracken to smell, but the moment Mr Kingston mentioned it, Janet knew it was there and she could smell it too. She knew too of the other things that were there, the rabbits, the birds and the squirrels.

The nightingale, whose song was the cue for their entrance, began to trill. Janet caught a quick, frightened breath. Basil Kingston put an arm round her shoulders.

'Look up, daughter. Nightingales are in the trees, not on the ground. It's a lovely night to go painting in a wood. We'll have fun.'

He was quite right, it was fun. It seemed to Janet that she really was in a magic wood. Not once did she remember that Mr Kingston was an actor and she an actress. He was her father and she was his daughter. Because she felt like that the end was terrible. Her father was going away, he would never come back, she was never going to be a live daughter, the wood would go, and she would fade away with it. Basil Kingston had to hum a song as he went off and Margaret was supposed to count to a hundred, by which time he said he would come back. But the wood was growing darker and the humming voice was out of earshot. Margaret could no longer count because she was too afraid, she was so afraid that she could hardly get out her words. Even the trees seemed to be fading. Everything was going. It was with a despairing gasp that she said her last line.

There was complete silence for a moment after the curtain had come down, then there was a roar like the sea on a stormy night. Mr Kingston caught hold of Janet's hand.

'Come along, daughter. We've got to go on and bow.'

When the play was over Janet found she was a success. It was difficult to make a success in a part like Margaret, which everybody knew so well, but the part fitted her as it could never have fitted Sally. With her rather coltish movements, her brown hair and charming, but not pretty, face, she was what Sir J. M. Barrie had intended Margaret to be, everybody's dream-daughter. When the curtain had been up and down several times Mr Kingston said:

'This time we'll bow just by ourselves, and we'll see which of us can bow best to your mother.'

Janet gave him a startled look, but she had no time to ask him what he meant. There was such a lot of applause for that curtain that they took another before they took the final curtain with the whole company. At the end of that curtain Mr Kingston made a nice little speech thanking everybody, then he stopped the applause by holding up his hand.

'I want to tell you a story. Many of you, I think, watching the play tonight, have guessed a secret; this face and this voice could only belong to one family.' He stepped back and took Janet by the hand and led her forward. 'This is the fifth generation of the Billingtons. Judy Billington's daughter.'

The next morning Janet sat by Sally's bed.

'How did you know, Sally? Mr Glay told me you told him.'

'Mrs Allison. She came to see me while I was waiting for the operation. I said I was afraid you were too scared to act and she laughed. She said "Not with that blood in her veins." Then she told me.'

Janet leaned back in her chair.

'All the Billingtons have been actors, as you know, but when my mother, Judy Billington, gave up acting to marry Dad, she promised she wouldn't encourage her children to act. She didn't. My brother Lawrence, luckily, wanted to be a pianist. I think she had always guessed about me. She signed my contract without a word. She cried when she heard I was to play Margaret, she was so pleased.'

'What did your father say when he found out?'

'He came to see me act the second night. All the family were there. Grandfather Billington and Grandmother, and Uncle Andrew. Mum and Lawrence were at the first night, of course.'

'Your uncle, the film star?'

'Yes. And my aunts. They're all actresses, you know. Dad wouldn't sit with them. He sat alone in the dress circle. I was awfully nervous.'

'What did he say afterwards?'

'He waited till Mum brought me home. Then he said, "All right. I lose. You can't stop a Billington."'

Coralie

Angus Barford, known to everybody as A.B., was sitting at his desk in his luxurious office in the vast building which housed Parthenon Films. In front of him, pencil at the ready, sat Stephanie his secretary, but no letter was dictated, and this was so unusual that Stephanie cleared her throat to remind him she was still there. A.B. looked up and smiled.

'Sorry. I'm afraid the letters will have to wait, I've things on my mind.'

'Don't I know it,' thought Stephanie, 'it's Coralie again. This will be a lesson to him not to put child film stars under long contracts.' But out loud she said, 'Will you see Mr Sholsky?'

A.B. nodded.

'Send him in.'

Adrian Sholsky came into the office with the assured air not only of Parthenon Films' leading director, but of a close friend of A.B.'s. He sank into the chair Stephanie had just left.

'Coralie, her aunt and her agent are in the waiting room.'

'I know,' said A.B. 'I've got to see them, but I haven't decided what to say.'

'How about the truth,' Adrian suggested.

A.B. doodled on his blotting paper.

'I had a talk with the legal boys last night, we can't break Coralie's contract, they're willing she should play the part.'

Adrian made an impatient movement.

'But am I willing to direct her? Granted she's clever and granted she's a box-office draw, but she's a bad-mannered little wretch, whose airs and graces upset the other actors.'

A.B. went on doodling.

'Suppose ... and mind you I only said suppose, the other directors insist on her being used in *Lavender's Blue*, for remember she's an expensive item to have around doing nothing ... does that mean you won't direct *Lavender's Blue?*'

Adrian ran his fingers through his hair, while he thought.

'I ought to say yes to that, but I don't know. It's such a good story, and the rest of the cast should be perfect, especially old Beatrice Stayne ... but she'll never stand for Coralie's star stuff.'

A.B. nodded.

'I've thought of that, and I've had an idea. Coralie's aunt and Ben Reubens her agent can pretend as much as they like, but they are scared stiff you won't use her in this film.'

'What do they expect?' Adrian growled. 'She was insufferable while I was making that last picture, and we had trouble, but if she behaves badly in this film Beatrice Stayne simply won't take it.'

'I know,' A.B. agreed, 'but it's not Coralie's fault, poor kid, it's that aunt who makes an absolute fool of her. But if I'm right and Ben Reubens would do anything to prevent her being dropped from *Lavender's Blue*, we might keep the aunt out of the studio, and that is stage one of an idea I have simmering.'

'Who are you planning should look after Coralie instead of the aunt?'

A.B. pressed a button and spoke into the intercom.

'Would you send Doctor Smith and Doctor Jakes in please.'

Adrian raised his eyebrows.

'Who on earth . . . ?'

A.B. smiled.

'Wait and see. You're in for a surprise.'

The door opened and two women were shown in. Both had grey hair; one was long and thin with search-ing eyes, the other short, plump and cosy.

'Adrian,' said A.B. introducing the Doctors, 'These two ladies were responsible for the education of Pauline Fossil.'

'And her sisters,' Doctor Jakes added, 'you can't sep-arate the Fossils. Pauline's coming over in a week or two you know, just to spend a holiday with her sister Petrova.'

Adrian clasped first Doctor Jakes and then Doctor Smith by the hand.

'I heard she was coming, and I'm hoping to have a sight of her. But we must have met. Didn't you ever come on the set when Pauline was in *Charles the Exile?*'

Doctor Jakes shook her head.

'No. Miss Brown or Nana brought Pauline to the studio.'

'But Doctor Jakes coached Pauline in the part,' Doctor Smith put in.

'Literature is my subject,' Doctor Jakes explained, 'but I'm fond of history. I remember so well the day Pauline came home from the film test you had given her, and rushed into my room saying "Tell me all about Charles the Second's sister Henrietta".'

A.B. went back to his desk.

'These ladies have retired, Adrian, but I'm trying to persuade them to take over the education and the chaperoning of Coralie during the run of *Lavender's Blue*.'

'If you do,' Adrian said to the Doctors, 'that is if A.B. can make Coralie's aunt agree to the idea, you'll have your hands full.'

Doctor Jakes nodded.

'We know. Mr Barford explained everything.'

Adrian looked at A.B.

'You're up to something.'

A.B. smiled.

'Something that you'll know about all in good time, and which if it works will bring back the nice Coralie we once knew.' He pressed a bell. 'Show the Doctors round, Adrian, while I see Coralie, her aunt and Ben Reubens.'

It was not prettiness which had made Coralie's face as well known as Princess Alexandra's, but something more enduring. She had an elfin quality plus friendliness, 'the sort of daughter we should all like to own' a critic had written about her. Coralie would have been shocked if she had known what every man attached to the studio had said when they read that. She had been born the warm-hearted child she looked; as a baby she had smiles for everyone, and had friends in every house in the neighbourhood in which she lived. Then her father and mother had been killed in a car accident, and she had been adopted by an aunt and uncle. A year later a talent scout had spotted her, and she had been given a small part in a film. By the time she was seven she was a star. If she had been wisely looked after, being a film star need not have altered her, but she was not wisely looked after. Her uncle fought hard to keep the Coralie he knew and loved, but Coralie's aunt would not let him. All her life she had longed to be somebody, not just a housewife, and through Coralie she was somebody and she adored it, so year by year she spoilt the child who had made her somebody, until no one could remember the Coralie everyone had loved.

A.B. asked his three visitors to sit. Then because it was a belief of his that when something had to be done, it was best to get it over with, he said:

'I've been discussing the part of Judy in *Lavender's*

Blue with Adrian Sholsky, and we have agreed it will not be the right part for you, Coralie.'

Coralie's aunt, who looked like a well-upholstered arm-chair, turned a purplish red.

'Not the right part! But it's perfect for her. Why the moment I heard you'd bought the book, I said to Coralie "You were born to play Judy".'

Ben Reubens interrupted her.

'Let's have the cards on the table, Mr Barford. Coralie's under contract, and she'd be fine as Judy, what's the trouble?'

A.B. looked directly at Coralie.

'Though you gave a good performance in your last picture, I've had complaints about your manner to the other artists.'

Coralie looked sulky.

'Just because I'm only fourteen, the grown-up actors don't treat me as a star, even when my billing's miles bigger than theirs.'

'It's true, A.B.,' said Coralie's aunt. 'Stand up for yourself, darling, I said, that's the only way to make them know who's who.'

A.B. turned to Ben Reubens.

'We shall be sorry not to have Coralie in the picture, but I can't have another cast upset.'

Ben Reubens could feel A.B. was holding something back.

'You've got an alternative?'

A.B. believed, when he had to strike a blow, in it being a good one. He looked at Coralie's aunt.

'Yes. I don't want you in the studio. If Coralie plays Judy, and mind you there's a big "if", we want her educated and chaperoned by teachers of our choosing.'

Coralie's aunt looked like a kettle that was going to boil over.

'I never heard anything so disgraceful.'

Coralie glared at A.B.

'I won't go to the studio without my aunt, and I don't want a new governess. The last one I had was all right.'

Ben Reubens gave A.B. an expressive look, which translated meant 'Leave this to me. I'll handle the aunt. Believe me, I'm not having Coralie lose this part for a woman like that.'

It was a very cross Coralie that turned up at the studio for the first day's shooting. When they had a child in a film the studio arranged that the scenes with which they were concerned, except during school holidays, were shot in the afternoons so they had undisturbed mornings for lessons. A room was set apart for a schoolroom, and there Coralie first met Doctor Jakes and Doctor Smith, for though normally they would call for her in a car belonging to the company, for this first morning her uncle had brought her to the studio.

'You may as well know,' said Coralie, 'that I'm not allowed to be bothered too much about lessons, the doctor told my aunt.'

'We shall not bother you,' said Doctor Jakes. 'Our time is too valuable.'

'So we only use it,' Doctor Smith explained, 'on those who wish to learn.'

Coralie, though she did not show it, felt awkward. All the governesses she had so far had, and there had been plenty, had been rather excited at being chosen to teach her, and she had done what she liked with them. Never had she learned from intelligent, highly trained women.

'What are we starting with?' she asked sourly.

'Obviously,' said Doctor Jakes, 'an examination paper. We can't teach you until we know what standard you have reached.'

The examination paper was not really difficult, but there were several questions Coralie could not answer.

When she had done as much as she could, she pushed her papers across to Doctor Jakes.

'That's all I know; people like me can't be expected to learn things like ordinary girls.'

Coralie started proper lessons the next morning, both the Doctors working hard to make up the deficiencies in her education, and since both were brilliant teachers, Coralie worked harder than she had worked for any of her other governesses. But as if to make up for being fairly good in the mornings she was particularly bumptious in the afternoons. Adrian had a hard job to soothe down the other actors, for 'That horrible girl', 'That conceited little moppet', 'Big-headed Coralie' and other such expressions growled round the studio.

'You must do something about that young woman,' old Beatrice Stayne told Adrian. 'I'm not accustomed to being spoken to rudely by a chit of a girl.'

'I know you're not,' said Adrian, for Dame Stayne was a great theatrical personage, 'but be patient. A.B. has a plan which may knock the conceit out of her, and you're part of it.'

Beatrice Stayne looked across the set to where the Doctors were sitting.

'Are they part of it too?'

Adrian nodded.

That afternoon a scene was shot between the grandmother of the story and Judy the granddaughter. It was an important scene for during it the audience had to read in the grandmother's face that for the first time she was worried about the way Judy was being brought up, and was facing the fact she would have to interfere. The grandmother was the part played by Beatrice Stayne.

Adrian had worked out every move and he rehearsed the scene even more carefully than usual, but giving so much of his attention to Beatrice Stayne that Coralie felt slighted.

'I don't like the position I'm in at the end of this scene, Adrian,' she said to draw attention to herself. 'I ought to be facing the camera not walking out of the door.'

Adrian's voice was like ice.

'That's the way I want it.'

'But it's all wrong,' Coralie argued. 'It's my scene.'

'That,' suggested Beatrice Stayne, 'is arguable.'

'It's not arguable at all,' said Adrian. 'It's the grandmother's scene. Now let's get on.'

Coralie gave in but with a bad grace, and under her breath she muttered, 'Judy's the star of this story, not the grandmother,' and both Beatrice Stayne and Adrian heard her.

That afternoon's shooting was the beginning of trouble for Coralie. Because she had a natural sense of timing, was easily directed, and very photogenic, she had seldom before had any trouble with her film parts. Sometimes a scene had taken a lot of working at, but in the end she had always got somewhere near what her director wanted. But from the day of her scene with

Beatrice Stayne, things began to go wrong. Not that Coralie felt she was wrong, it was, she thought, Adrian's attitude to her and the attitude of everyone on the set that was the trouble.

'No, Coralie,' Adrian would say in rather a weary voice as if he were tired of saying it, 'You aren't getting the right inflection.' Or 'What's the matter with you, Coralie? You must try harder.' And each time she was pulled up Coralie sensed the cast and studio exchanging looks and sighing. But so secure was she in the knowledge of her success and popularity, that at first she shrugged away Adrian's complaints as 'He must have got out of bed the wrong side'. Then as day after day the criticisms of her acting went on even she became slightly worried. It could not be anything to do with her. She was Coralie the child film star. It must be everybody else who was wrong. But deep inside her she felt stabs of anxiety. Her comfort was her aunt.

'Don't worry, pettums,' her aunt said when Coralie told her how difficult Adrian was being. 'It's that old woman Beatrice Stayne, I expect. He's playing up to her by being cross with you. Keep your chin up and show them who's the star.'

Coralie kept her chin up and tried never to let

Adrian or anybody else know she was worried. Then one day A.B. sent for her.

'I hear you are having trouble over playing Judy,' he said. 'So I'm giving you tomorrow off to think about the part.'

'I don't want a day off.' Coralie was cross because she was scared. 'I'm liking playing Judy.'

A.B. spoke gently.

'It's Adrian who has to like your playing. Now run away and have a quiet day and think, my child, not about yourself but about Judy.'

Although Coralie did not say so, even to her aunt, she had a horrid day and was very glad the next morning to be back at the studio. It had been so odd while making an expensive film to give an artist who was needed a day off, that it made her wonder what lay behind it. Then just as lessons had started there was an interruption which brought her suspicions to a head. A page boy came to the schoolroom door.

'Mr Sholsky's compliments, and the rushes are being shown. He says if one of you ladies can come now, he'll have them run through again for the other lady later.'

Doctor Smith, as if she was expecting the summons, got up and went out, and Coralie was left alone with

Doctor Jakes. There was a cold frightened feeling in her inside. All the cast saw the previous day's shots, called rushes, daily during the lunch break, but none of yesterday's rushes concerned her and therefore the Doctors. It must be yesterday's shots that were being shown. Why should the Doctors be sent for to look at rushes of scenes filmed on the day she was away? Coralie pretended she was listening to Doctor Jakes's geography lesson, but she wasn't, her mind was twisting and turning. Something was up. What? Suddenly she could bear it no longer: making the excuse that she wanted a handkerchief from her dressing-room she rushed out of the schoolroom. Doctor Jakes closed the atlas and smiled.

Coralie was not allowed to go about the studio alone, but disregarding this she ran to the little cinema where the rushes of *Lavender's Blue* were shown. She opened the soundproof door and slipped in. It was the close-up of Beatrice Stayne that was showing; her clever old face was looking towards the door. 'Run along now, Judy,' her voice said, but her eyes were saying 'I must do something about this child'. Then the camera panned to the door, and Coralie watched to see herself as Judy going out of the room. Then her heart felt as if it had missed a beat, for the Judy in the doorway was not her, it was Pauline Fossil.

Coralie never knew how she got out of the cinema and into her own dressing-room. Then she shut the door, and not turning on any lights, crept into a corner, and lying on the floor cried and cried. It was too awful. It was the end of everything. It had been advertised she was to play Judy. How could she face it when the news broke she was not good enough, that Pauline Fossil had been brought back from America to take her place? At first she blamed everybody, A.B. for not letting her aunt come to the studio, then Adrian, then Beatrice Stayne, but presently a tiny voice whispered, 'Perhaps it was your fault. Aren't you a rather conceited idiot? So conceited that it showed when you were playing Judy?'

Doctor Jakes's voice pierced through Coralie's sobs.

'My dear child, what are you doing here in the dark?'

Coralie sat up. Her voice wailed like the wind when a storm is rising.

'You know what's happened. They're using Pauline Fossil instead of me.'

Doctor Jakes turned on the lights. Then she sat down at Coralie's dressing table.

'I know nothing of the sort. I know they would like to use her, but Pauline I understand is under contract to another studio.'

'Then why did they shoot her in my scene?'

'I can imagine poor Mr Sholsky hoped he might get Pauline, and it must have been a nice change for him and for Miss Stayne, even for a day, to work with a real artist who was humble about her work and pleasant to be with.'

There was a pause while Coralie took this in. Then choking down her sobs, she whispered, 'I suppose I have been hateful.'

Doctor Jakes nodded.

'You have, but you're only fourteen, there's time to improve.'

After a pause Coralie said, 'How would you start showing you meant to try if you were me?'

Doctor Jakes considered.

'I'd ask to see Mr Barford, and if he would see me I'd tell him I knew I'd been a conceited silly little girl, and get him to give me another chance.'

'I can't go like this,' said Coralie. 'Look at my face.'

Doctor Jakes picked up a hairbrush.

'Perhaps a little brushing wouldn't hurt, but Mr Barford won't mind those swollen eyes, in fact I think he'll be glad to see them if they mean, as I am sure they do, that they've washed away a lot of conceit.'

When Coralie had gone Doctor Jakes went to a

studio telephone. She put through a call, and asked to speak to Pauline Fossil.

'Thank you my dear,' she said, when Pauline came on the line, 'for giving up one day of your holiday. But it was well worth it, for I believe it's worked.'

Ordinary Me

The Posters were a successful family. Mr Poster had swum the Channel when he was a young man, and won two hundred pounds for doing it, and the sort of dogged tenacity needed by a Channel swimmer he seemed to have passed on to his children. Mrs Poster each year since she had married had won prizes at the local shows for her cakes and pickles. Any woman who can go on winning prizes year after year for her cooking must not only be a good cook, but full enough of the competitive spirit not to mind what the other competitors are saying about her; this quality Mrs Poster had handed on. As a result the Poster home in Surbiton burgeoned with cups, and Mr Poster, who was a church sidesman, handed round the collection plate on Sundays looking, as well he might, every inch the proud father.

George, the eldest of the Poster children, was captain of cricket at his school, and was expected to play for England. Alec was junior boxing champion for all England. Denise was at a ballet school, and was showing such promise that she was already spoken of as a future Fonteyn. Kathy at ten was already a most promising tennis player. But there was one blot on this picture of success. It was Alice. Alice was fourteen. A year younger than Alec and a year older than Denise, and she shone at nothing, absolutely nothing at all.

'Don't bother, dear,' her mother said, 'it's nice to have one stay-at-home daughter, and I'm glad of your help.'

But Alice was sure even that was not true. When the boys were out boxing and playing games, Denise at a class and Kathy practising in the back garden with a ball, it would have been comforting if she could have produced a cake as good as those made by her mother and said 'I made this.' But it would not have been true, for try as she would Alice was a heavy-handed cook.

But though Alice might not shine at anything, she had qualities which, though she did not know it, were very much her own. She thought her brothers and sisters called her 'Poor old Alice' because they were sorry for her; it never struck her the title was meant affectionately. She thought when George shouted to her to find something it was because he knew she was the only one with time to look for things; she never thought George was relying on her. When Alec brought her things to mend, and stayed while she sewed to tell her about the boxing, she supposed he thought poor old Alice was the only member of the family with time to mend and time to listen; it never crossed her mind he counted on her, and liked telling her things. It was the same when she darned Denise's ballet shoes while Denise told her what went on in her ballet school. Alice thought Denise was trying to amuse her; she never guessed how glad Denise was to have an interested listener. Even when she threw balls at Kathy's tennis racket it never struck Alice she was being good-natured; she thought Kathy was allowing her to join in her highly skilled game. So, not knowing where her gifts lay, Alice, if it had not been for her secret, would have had an inferiority complex.

The secret began two years before the start of this story. It was just before Christmas and Alice had come home from school by a different route, because she had heard of a store where, gossip had it, a special kind of tobacco pouch could be bought, made in the shape of a swimmer, which she thought would make a most suitable Christmas present for her father. She did not find the tobacco pouch, but in the store that was supposed to sell it and did not, she met a girl who put an idea into her head. The department that was supposed to sell the tobacco pouches was called 'Notions', and arriving at the counter at the same time as Alice was a thin girl with big brown eyes and a lot of reddish hair. This girl and Alice began to ask for what each wanted at the same moment, and of course that made them laugh and speak to each other. What the other girl had wanted she could not get either, so the two had moved away from the Notions counter together, and as they walked they had exchanged information.

The girl said her name was Harriet Johnson, that she did not go to school, but did lessons with her great friend Lalla Moore so that they could work together at the rink.

Alice knew nothing at that time about skating.

'The rink?' she asked. 'What sort of skating do you do? Roller?'

Harriet looked quite shocked.

'No, ice skating. It's glorious. There are examinations, so you are always working for something new and difficult. Lalla is a marvellous exhibition skater. You ought to hear the way she's cheered, and she gets lots of lovely bouquets.'

In that second Alice stopped being herself and was an exhibition skater; she did not think about the learning part, but only about the cheering audiences and the bouquets. How wonderful to surprise the family, at last they would be proud of her.

'How do you start to learn?' she asked Harriet.

'It's easy,' Harriet said. 'You go to the rink, that costs two-and-six a session, and you hire boots, they cost two shillings. Tell you what, if you'd like to try I'll help you. Just let me know when you're going to be there, I'll give you my address so you can send me a postcard.'

That was how it started. As it happened, thanks to a rich godfather and other tips, Alive had over five pounds that Christmas, so she had plenty of money to go skating and for lessons as well. It had not even been difficult to keep it a secret she was learning to skate, for during the holidays she had school friends she went out with, and sometimes during the term she visited them on Saturdays, so when she was out that was where her family supposed she was. There was family grumbling that she was never at home when she was most wanted, but Alice thought that was the others trying to be nice to the family failure. 'But they needn't always be ashamed of me,' she promised herself, 'some day I'll show them.'

Harriet more than kept her promise, she gave up time to help Alice, and when Alice could totter round the rink unaided she arranged she should have a weekly lesson from Max Lindblom, the best of all the teachers.

'She's not ever going to be your sort of skater, Max, but all her family are fearfully good at something, and she's a very hard worker, so perhaps if you teach her she'll be good enough some day to do a not very difficult solo at a gala. That's what she wants, so her family will be proud of her.'

Max looked across the rink at Alice. At that time she was on the plump side and was going through a spotty period. Her skating was earnest and careful.

'It is no good, Harriet, for you I would do much, but I can never make a skater of that child.'

'Of course you can, you can make a skater of anybody. Please say you'll try.'

Max tried, but two years later, in spite of his trying and Alice's hard work, Alice was still a below-average skater, and Harriet had to face the fact. She discussed the situation with her friend Lalla.

'It's so odd. She doesn't seem to know she'll never be any good. She still thinks if she works she'll be able to be an exhibition skater which will make her family proud of her.'

There had been a time when Lalla had been expected by everybody except Max Lindblom to be a world amateur champion, whereas she could only pass her figure-skating tests by the grimmest application; now her ambition and her talent all pointed to her becoming a professional, for she was a beautiful free skater. But because she had known a long period of time when she had tried to make herself believe she could be something she could not be, she could sympathise with Alice in a more understanding way than Harriet could, for Harriet looked like becoming the world amateur champion almost without wishing for it.

'Leave it to me,' Lalla said, 'I'll think of a way to help her. So don't fuss.'

Some months passed before Lalla saw a way to help Alice, but she did not forget that she had promised to. Then one morning when Harriet arrived at Lalla's house for her lessons, Lalla was waiting in the hall for her. She dragged Harriet into the dining-room, which was empty.

'I've found a way to help Alice.'

'How?'

'You remember I did an exhibition to help refugees last year at that rink in north London?'

Harriet nodded.

'You did "The Butterfly".'

'That's right. Well, the man who manages that rink rang up last night to ask if I could help him out tomorrow. The star skater he had invited for this year has mumps. Well, I couldn't because I'd promised Max I'd never give exhibitions anywhere twice, but I said I knew a marvellous skater who would skate for him.'

'Who?' asked Harriet.

'Alice of course. I gave him her name and said I could promise him she was good, and would do it. He was awfully grateful because of course time's short.'

Harriet, horrified, clutched hold of Lalla.

'Have you gone mad? Alice isn't marvellous, she couldn't give an exhibition – you know she couldn't.'

Lalla sighed at what she thought was Harriet's stupidity.

'She isn't going to, idiot, you said she wanted to make her family proud of her. Well, she can, only it won't be her they'll watch, it'll be me.'

Harriet still did not understand.

'But how? Everybody knows you by sight, and anyway her family would know it wasn't Alice skating.'

'You can be silly,' Lalla complained. 'Do you think I

hadn't thought of that? I'll do my white cat dance, no one'll know who's behind the cat mask.'

Everything took a lot of planning. First Alice had to be got hold of and told what was planned. Lalla and Harriet sent a telegram to her school, and told her without fail to meet them at the rink at five. Then somebody grown-up had to be used, for Lalla had to have help to go out in the evening. There were two people to choose between, Miss Goldthorpe who taught the two girls lessons, and Lalla's old nurse Nana, who was still with her to look after her clothes. In the end they chose Nana, for she was easier to fool than Miss Goldthorpe; she was told she was going with Lalla to a charity skating gala, as Lalla had a friend skating.

'Who is that, dear?' Nana asked without being really interested.

'Alice Poster,' said Lalla casually, 'you must have seen me talking to her.'

'I daresay, dear,' Nana agreed. 'But there's so many you know.'

The next problem was clothes. What excuse had Lalla to take her white cat dress in the car when she was only going to be in the audience? Then Harriet had an idea.

'Take it to Alice today. After all, she'll have to have

a costume to show her family, they'll know she couldn't skate in ordinary clothes.'

'I hope they don't make her try it on then,' said Lalla, 'for though she's about the same age as me, she's taller.'

Harriet laughed.

'I wouldn't think she knows how to put on a tutu or tights, and anyway she'd look awfully odd wearing them, she just isn't the type.'

The great stumbling block to Lalla's plan was Alice herself. When told what was planned she turned quite white.

'Oh no, we couldn't do that. I mean, everyone would know you weren't me, Lalla. I mean, look at you, and anyway you're a simply marvellous skater, nothing would make my family believe I could skate like you.'

Lalla loathed having any plan she made interfered with.

'Don't talk rubbish. It's all arranged – why, you're in the programme.'

Alice turned desperately to Harriet.

'Do make her see, Harriet. It's heavenly of Lalla to try and help, but my family couldn't be fooled. Lalla's too good a skater.'

'It's too late now,' Harriet explained, 'everything's

fixed – and honestly I don't think you need fuss, people look so different in masks.'

'Not that different,' Alice said gloomily. 'Nobody could think Lalla's gorgeous legs were mine.'

Lalla thought Alice was being tiresome.

'Stop fussing. Take the clothes home and show them to your family, but don't put them on of course, for they won't fit, and I'll meet you in your dressing-room at seven o'clock. You'll probably have to hide somewhere while I'm skating, we'll think of that when we get there.'

Alice turned pleadingly to Harriet.

'If I've got to pretend, you will come with me, won't you, Harriet? I'll never dare ask where I'm to dress and all that if I'm alone.'

But Harriet, though she would have loved it, could not help.

'I'm awfully sorry. It's a family birthday, I can't possibly go out.'

To say the Posters were surprised is an understatement.

'You skating! A solo!' said Mr Poster, 'I'll believe that when I see it.'

Mrs Poster gaped at the nylon tights and the tutu.'

'It's nice of your friend to lend them, dear, but are you sure they fit? They don't look your size.'

Denise examined the tutu.

'It's beautifully made, but I believe Mum's right and it's too small. You'd better slip it on and let me look at you in it.'

The boys examined the white boots and skates.

'Of all the secretive types,' said George, 'it's you, Alice. Why didn't you tell us what you were up to?'

'Are you sure you can make it?' Alec asked. 'I mean I'll come and see you of course, if you can do it, but we don't want to watch you falling over.'

'Is it the white cat dance from *The Sleeping Princess*?' Denise wanted to know. 'Go on, you can show me the steps without the skates, can't you?'

It was Kathy who came to Alice's rescue.

'You want to surprise us, don't you, Alice? I think you'll be a lovely white cat.'

Thankfully Alice picked up Lalla's skates and boots, and the round box holding the cat costume.

'You're quite right, Kathy. You wait, all of you. I won't put on my things nor show you what I'm doing until tomorrow.'

'Better ring up for seats,' said Mr Poster when Alice

had gone out of the room, 'and no matter what you have to put off you're all coming. It's the first time our Alice has had a chance to shine, and nobody is going to say her family were not there to watch her.'

The next day a trembling Alice arrived at the rink where the gala was being held. Nervously she sidled in holding the dress box and the skates.

'Where do I dress?' she whispered to the commissionaire.

The commissionaire was an experienced rink doorkeeper. 'Doesn't look much like a skater,' he thought, 'but maybe for the show tonight they have girls standing about as pages and such.'

'What's your name?' he asked.

Alice, from where she was standing, could see her name at the top of the list he was holding.

'That's me,' she said in a nervous squeak.

The doorkeeper thought of the magnificent bouquet of carnations delivered earlier, of the private dressing-room and the great ones who had occupied it, and looking at Alice he did not quite succeed in hiding his surprise.

'Oh! You're Miss Poster. Come this way please. I'll let the manager know you've arrived.'

Alice, alone in her dressing-room, looked round like a hunted hare. What was she to say to the manager if he came in to see her before Lalla arrived? If she was Lalla what would she be doing now? What did managers expect skating stars to be doing when they came to call? Having not the faintest idea of the answers to these questions, Alice sat down on the straight little chair at the dressing table, crossed her feet, folded her hands in her lap, and, to keep her mind off her problems, began reciting in her head the names and dates of England's kings and queens.

Alice had just reached Henry the Eighth when there was a knock on the door and the manager came in. Used to Lalla, he expected a skating friend of hers to look much as she did, so he had a shock when he saw Alice, for Lalla who was rich was beautifully dressed, which poor Alice coming in the middle of a large family was not. Lalla had been a success since she was a child, and she had the secure air of the successful; Alice's feeling of inferiority had never been worse than it was that night.

The manager, stifling his dismay, managed to smile.

'Alice Poster? This is good of you. Now, have you everything you want?'

Alice looked round helplessly. What did skating stars want?

'Oh yes, thank you.'

The manager opened a programme. Horrified, Alice stared at her name.

'We've put you on just after eight. Will you come to the rink entrance as soon as you are called.'

Alice licked her lips.

'Yes, I will dress as quickly as possible and come when I'm called.'

'As you know, we're using records, have you got yours?'

Alice was expecting that question. She handed him Lalla's record, which was in the bottom of the dress box.

'Here it is.'

The manager took it and went to the door.

'I must leave you, for I expect you should be dressing, for time's getting on. Good luck, my dear.' He went out and shut the door.

'Time's getting on!' Alice stared at her watch. Time was getting on, it was ten minutes past seven. Where was Lalla? She had sworn she would be here at seven o'clock. Perhaps she had better unpack Lalla's dress, for she would be in a hurry when she arrived. She hung the tutu on a peg, laid the tights over a chair, put

Lalla's skates on the floor, and the cat head-dress on the dressing table. She tried to do all this slowly, but panic had hold of her and she could not slow down. Soon it was quarter past, then twenty past. Something had happened. Lalla was not coming. Perspiration beaded Alice's forehead. What was she to do? Ought she to try putting on Lalla's clothes? But what good would that do, she could not skate a solo, she could only do the simplest figures and those not very well.

Suddenly the full horror of her position swept over her. Fool that she had been ever to want to shine at anything. Oh, what would she not give now to be at home darning Denise's shoes, throwing balls to Kathy, finding things for George, or mending things for Alec. That was what she was good at and was meant to do, she had no place in this terrifying show world. She laid her head on the dressing table and sobbed.

Five minutes later Lalla dashed in.

'Oh goodness, you must have been scared. Imagine! The car broke down. Quick, help me to change, and the moment they call me hide in that cupboard until I come back. Oh, you'd better put on this dressing-gown, I brought it with me on purpose. That's in case someone comes to say thank you before you would have had time to change.'

Hidden in the cupboard Alice heard Lalla clatter out of the door. Presently she heard Lalla's cat music, and later still Lalla's applause, which was enormous. Then suddenly Lalla, half-hidden behind carnations, was back.

'Quick, help me change, they were a gorgeous audience, didn't you wish I was really you?'

Alice unfastened Lalla's tutu.

'No. I knew in those awful minutes when I thought you weren't coming, how glad I am to be just ordinary me.'

Cows Eat Flowers

Almost all the girls at Cornwall Secondary Modern had illnesses. Not just influenza and bronchitis but proper hospital affairs like tonsils or appendicitis. Those who did not get ill broke bones or had crooked backs. It was, Edna thought, a cruel shame the way she – and almost she alone – came up for school medical after school medical and nothing the matter with her. Even her teeth never had anything wrong with them and she was practically the only girl in the school who could say that. Somehow her mum managed to get to the school for her medicals, which was not easy with Dad always in bed, but it was a waste of time.

'I don't know how you do it, Mrs Clark,' the lady doctor would say admiringly, 'but as usual there's nothing the matter with Edna.'

It was not the same with Edna's brother Jim, who went to the Junior mixed. Everything that could be had Jim had – usually badly. When he had his tonsils out he had to have a blood transfusion. When it was his appendix they put tubes in him. When it was measles he was so bad they had to take him to hospital. Even chickenpox he had so severely that he was sent to isolation in case it was smallpox. As a result, on so many occasions she had lost count of them, Edna had watched Jim being packed up and sent for convalescence. And there was she, eleven-plus past, almost twelve and had never put a foot out of London.

The maddening thing was that Jim either would not or could not appreciate his enormous good luck. To him going for convalescence meant something to be endured. The reason was that puny little Jim was a cockney to each one of his miserable sinews, so he thought every second spent away from the London streets unmitigated hell.

'But, Jim, you was at the sea. What's the sea like, Jim?' To which Jim would answer:

'Just a lot of water.'

'But you swam in it,' Edna would plead. 'Didn't you see seaweed and that?'

'I swam of course, I was made to,' Jim agreed. 'But come to that so did horses, I seen 'em.'

It was even more aggravating when Jim was sent to the country, for to visit the country was to Edna to enter Paradise.

'Is it right, Jim, that flowers grow in the country what anyone can pick?'

Jim, bored but willing to be helpful, thought back through a blur of ox-eyed daisies, buttercups and dog roses.

'I suppose you could, if you wanted, but I never.'

It was an awful thing that Jim, with all his opportunities, cared for nothing but towns. That the shabbiest back street was more interesting to him than any seaside beach or country lane. However, he was a kind boy and hardship had drawn him and Edna together. Sick benefit for Dad, who was what Mum described as 'proper eaten with that arthritis', plus public assistance, which was supposed to ensure there was no want in the Welfare State, meant there were the barest necessities of life in the Clark home. When you can't compete at all with the neighbourhood children whose fathers are working and who therefore take things for granted, like washing machines and the telly, it does draw you together. As a result, in his inarticulate way, Jim tried to tell Edna the kind of things she wanted to know.

'The country's miles of fields and that; of course there's flowers what people could pick only they don't because there's not many people about. But cows eat 'em, I seen 'em.'

'Cows eat flowers'! It was that statement of Jim's which haunted Edna. Here was she who had never once picked flowers yet cows ate them. Once, just once, she had owned a plant. It had been a double daisy and it was Jim who had given it to her. His teacher had planted a trough of flowers to grow on the classroom window ledge. There was a double daisy over and she had asked who would like it. At once every hand in the class shot up. 'Me, Miss. Please me, Miss.' She was fond of Jim, he was so frail and so courageous, so she gave him the daisy. Proudly he had brought it home and given it to Edna.

'She said to plant it in a pot and put it outside the window.'

She didn't have a pot or compost, but that did not mean Edna let her double daisy die. A few streets away there was a church with a small square of sooty earth in front of it. There was a railing round the church but

the bars were wide enough for Edna's not very fat arms
to get through. So with the help of a fork she dug a little
hole and planted her daisy.

'No one knows,' she whispered to the plant as she
patted it into place, 'but you're mine, my very own.'

Two months later when the daisy had a few sooty
little red button flowers Edna had the exquisite pleasure
of looking at it through the railings. She hoped the daisy
would live through the winter and flower next year but,
probably discouraged by the poor earth, it vanished.

It was March when the miracle happened. The headmistress after prayers held up her hand to stop the front
row marching off to their classroom.

'I want the name of any girl in this school who has
not had a holiday out of London. I realise most of you
have not only been out of London but abroad, but if
there should be one of you who has never been away
please let me have your name.'

Edna did not suffer from false pride. You could not
really when you had always had less than anybody else,
so she wrote on a clean piece of paper 'Clark. Edna. Date
of birth April 22. Age last birthday 11', which was the

way they liked things written in school. Underneath: 'I never been out of London.'

The result of giving in that piece of paper was that Edna was startled by being summoned into the head-mistress's study.

'What you been up to?' the girl asked who brought the summons.

Edna struggled to remember.

'I can't think of anythin' what I done different to what I should.'

The headmistress's study was a very nice room. It had yellow walls and golden curtains, a brown sofa with gold cushions on it and on the desk was a vase of golden jonquils. Edna, who in the school was in no way distin-guished, had never been in the room before. She looked at the flowers in rapture. The headmistress thought her expression indicated stupidity.

'Oh Edna! This is Mrs Gleeson.'

That drew Edna away from the jonquils. She looked at Mrs Gleeson and recognised immediately what she was. She knew what that green coat and skirt, green hat and wine-coloured blouse meant. Mrs Gleeson was WVS – in the Women's Voluntary Service. Lovely ladies they were, she had often seen them taking dinner to old Mrs Potts in the block of flats up the road.

'How d'you do, Miss,' she said.

Mrs Gleeson smiled at Edna.

'Is it true you've never had a country holiday, Edna?'

Edna, having filled in all the answers on that piece of paper, thought this a silly question.

'Yes. That's what I wrote.'

'Would you like to go?'

Edna's face shone as if the rising sun was on it.

'Wouldn't I just!'

'Well, you shall go, then. Tell me, would you rather go to the country or to the sea?'

Edna took so long answering the headmistress felt she needed helping.

'Which would you prefer, Edna? Answer Mrs Gleeson.'

Edna was seeing fields of white daisies, hedges of pink roses and miles of yellow buttercups, all to be picked by anyone who wanted. At last she gasped, for such visions took away her breath:

'The country, please, Miss.'

After that the most wonderful things happened. It seemed that a holiday such as was planned for Edna could not be properly enjoyed in old clothes. Mrs Clark kept her children washed and patched but some of Edna's things were more darn than anything else. So, just as if they knew this, a WVS lady called for Edna and carted her off to what they called a clothing centre. There she was not only fitted out with new clothes from top to bottom but all the new clothes, except Wellingtons which had to be carried, were packed in a new suitcase with, in a little bag, a new toothbrush and a new face flannel. Such grandeur! Dad was so pleased when he saw it all that he cried, something he never did however bad the pain was.

Jim, from his immense experience, tried to put Edna wise as to what to expect.

'You'll have a lot of people looking after you fussing about what you eat, and havin' baths and that. You got to stand up for yourself.'

But where Edna was taken was not a bit like the places Jim had been to. Mrs Gleeson drove Edna – all dressed up in her new clothes – in her car.

'You're going to stay on a farm, Edna. It's in Kent and they grow cherries, which should be in blossom now.'

At the farm there was Mr Coomb, the farmer, and Mrs Coomb, the farmer's wife, both jolly and round, who seemed to care about nothing but the amount of food they could persuade Edna to eat, and that she spent every minute when she was not eating in the open air. There were lambs, puppies and a little foal, but everything for Edna, even her splendid clothes, was eclipsed by the flowers. Cherry blossom, miles and miles of it, white against the pale blue spring sky. Then up the road in a wood there were at first primroses and later bluebells.

'You can pick as many as you like,' said Mrs Coomb.

But Edna did not want to pick the flowers, she only wanted to look at them. Amazed, she said:

'I reckon there's always something in flower in these parts, ain't there?'

'Always,' Mrs Coomb agreed. 'I plant my garden so there is always a show.'

Edna studied Mrs Coomb's garden and learned the names of what grew.

Tulips, polyanthus, with peonies to come, and London Pride in the border with forget-me-nots and pansies.

'Dad and I were thinking,' Mrs Coomb said towards the end of Edna's visit, 'as you are so fond of flowers you should take some plants back. We'll only give you strong plants that will grow anywhere.'

Edna loved Mrs Coomb's garden and every plant growing in it. 'Not on your life,' she said to herself. 'I'm not taking nothin' from here. I'm not puttin' nothin' more in that church earth. I seen now how proper country flowers did oughter grow. That daisy what I 'ad never grew as it should.' Out loud she said:

'I don't want to take no plants back, thank you. I reckon they wouldn't like it where I hang out.'

The Coombs had become very fond of Edna. They knew about Dad's arthritis and how often Jim had to go on convalescence. They had shared Edna's pride in the lovely clothes the WVS had provided, and had seen that every garment had been given a proper outing. They knew what enormous pleasure a small window box could give a town dweller, so Mrs Coombs said:

'Don't you worry, Edna. The flowers I give you will settle down all right. Why if, as we hope, you come to stay next holiday you'll be bringing me a bunch of what you've grown. You see if you aren't.'

'No, thank you,' said Edna. 'I'd rather not take the plants, truly I would.'

'Don't you listen to her, me dear,' Mr Coomb told Mrs Coomb. 'You just pack her a nice bundle. She'll soon find somewhere to plant the stuff.'

Mrs Gleeson came to fetch Edna. She thought she had never seen such a change in a child, for Edna had a radiance about her that turned a rather plain little girl into a beauty. Mr Coomb and Mrs Coomb came out to the car, Mrs Coomb with a cardboard box in which were eggs, cream, butter, jam and honey. Edna had a large parcel of plants. Mr Coomb had Edna's suitcase and Wellingtons. He put the case and Wellingtons into the boot.

'I don't know what you're taking home, Edna,' he laughed, 'but from the weight of your case you might have got potatoes and vegetable marrows.'

On the way to London Mrs Gleeson heard about the holiday. The cherry blossom, the primroses, the bluebells, Mrs Coomb's garden and again the cherry blossom.

'And what about the clothes?' she asked. 'Had you got the right things?'

Edna turned and looked out of the window at the drab town streets they were passing. There was a pause while she swallowed a lump in her throat.

'Oh, they were smashing! I didn't ever have anything nice before. Does something for you havin' nice clothes, doesn't it?'

It was just as Edna said this that they came to a road block. A policeman stepped forward.

'Sorry, ma'am,' he said to Mrs Gleeson, 'There's been a big robbery. We have to stop all cars. Have you any luggage?'

'There's a case in the boot,' said Mrs Gleeson, 'and

on the back seat some plants and a parcel of eggs and things.'

It was as the policeman went to the boot that Edna screamed:

'You leave that case alone, copper. Nobody ain't going to open that but me.'

Mrs Gleeson was amazed that Edna, who had seemed such a nice child, could behave so badly.

'Edna, don't be silly, child. The constable has a right to open the case if he wants to.'

Edna shook off Mrs Gleeson's restraining hand, opened the car door and shot out. The policeman had the boot open but Edna flung herself across the case.

'Don't you dare touch. You 'aven't a warrant. I know me rights.'

The policeman and Mrs Gleeson pulled Edna, kicking and screaming, off the case.

'Sorry,' said the policeman, 'but I have my orders.'

'Of course,' Mrs Gleeson agreed. 'Open the case, Constable.'

The case was not locked. The policeman pressed down the two catches and the lid shot open. Inside there were no potatoes or vegetable marrows, there was not even Edna's new wardrobe, instead the case was full to the brim with rich Kent earth.

Edna sobbed so much that at first Mrs Gleeson could get nothing out of her, so she drove on in silence, but presently, through hiccuping sobs, the story came out.

'It weren't right to take them plants – not where I live. The earth by the church, the only place I could plant 'em, is mostly soot and cobwebs and that. I did 'ave a flower or two on me daisy, but it weren't like it should 'ave been. And I 'ad to plant it poking me arms through the bars. I couldn't do that with the plants Mrs Coomb give me.'

'What did you mean to do?'

Edna lowered her voice as if afraid someone might overhear.

'I'd have had to get Jim and his lot to help but I thought, after dark like, we could take along the earth and I could plant me plants in what they were used to.'

There was a long silence, then Mrs Gleeson said:

'Let's get this straight. You were bringing back all this earth to mix with the earth in front of the church?'

Edna nodded.

'It's just earth. I mean, nothin' is planted there.'

'What did you do with your new clothes?'

Edna tried to hold back a sob.

'I feel terrible about them. But I had to leave them. I done them up nice inside the mackintosh so they won't get wet. There's an apple tree that's hollow, Mr Coomb showed me, I put 'em inside that.'

Mrs Gleeson did not speak for some time.

'You'd better direct me to the church. It's no good taking all that earth home, is it?'

Edna was horrified.

'Not now we can't take it, it's daylight, we'd 'ave a copper on us quick as winkin'.'

Mrs Gleeson gave Edna a dig in the ribs with her elbow.

'Let's risk the copper.'

Edna was amazed. She liked Mrs Gleeson, she thought she was as nice as Mrs Coomb, which was saying a lot. But what she was meeting now was a new Mrs Gleeson – a fellow conspirator.

They arrived at the church. There was the sad little patch of dirty town earth, just as Edna had described it. There were the railings through which she had put her arms to plant the double daisy. Mrs Gleeson got out of the car and opened the gate in the railings. Then she helped Edna carry in the suitcase and tip out the earth. As best they could manage without a spade they spread out the good Kent loam.

'Now,' said Mrs Gleeson, 'we'll go and buy a trowel and a water can.'

Edna was sorry for Mrs Gleeson. A proper lady like she was needed looking after.

'We can't plant anything now. Let's come back when it's dark.'

Mrs Gleeson shook her head.

'No. I'm a lion of courage when I'm roused. We are going to put the plants in now and I don't care who sees us.'

'But what will you say if a copper comes?'

'Oh, just this is Edna who is making the desert rejoice and blossom as the rose.'

Edna looked admiringly at Mrs Gleeson.

'You aren't half a caution,' she said.

Andrew's Trout

Neither Andrew nor Angela could remember a time when they were not taken to watch their father fish. They always travelled in the van for Father and his brother, the children's Uncle Bob, had a vegetable stall in a London market, and the van was kept to carry the vegetables from the market.

Except on bank holidays the family went fishing only for the day. The stall wasn't cleared of vegetables until late Saturday afternoons. But on Easter, Whitsun and August bank holidays they packed a tent, a cooking stove and mattresses into the van and went off so early on the Sunday it was still dark, and came home very late on a Monday night. On Sundays their father fished in the canal water that lay close to London. But on bank holidays they would go down to Kent.

Angela and the children's mother were not interested in fishing; Andrew had been once but seemed to have gone off it. His father wondered why.

'Funny young Andrew not liking fishing like he did,' he would say to his wife. 'Keen as mustard he once was.'

'You know how boys are,' she would answer. 'Crazy on a thing one day and won't look at it the next. But I shouldn't wonder if he came back to it.'

The reason Andrew no longer talked fishing to his father was that what he now meant by 'fishing' was not what his father meant.

It had happened one August bank holiday. The water bailiff had been round looking at licences. Afterwards he sat down close to where Andrew was sitting to light his pipe.

'Why aren't you fishing?'

'There's only Dad's rod,' Andrew explained. 'I watch it for him when he goes to have a drink. He says he could catch a 17-pound perch here.'

'So he could I shouldn't wonder, and a fine fight the

perch would give him. But there's not many that size hereabouts.'

'I know,' Andrew agreed. 'Everything my dad catches, unless it's a big eel, he puts back. He says he likes to see the way they flick their tails as they make off, as if to say "Thanks, mate".'

'This fishing is all right, son, but what you want to get a chance at one day is fly fishing. That's real sport, that is.'

'Do you have a fly instead of paste?'

The bailiff shook his head.

'It's a different business altogether. The fly floats on the surface, you flick it down and then away again. It's like a real fly, see. And when you're lucky that's what a trout thinks it is and he snaps it up.'

Andrew was very vague about trout. He had never seen one or eaten one, he just knew there were such fish.

'Where do you get them?'

'Rivers. Often it's pools they like. Or maybe a lake. Quiet places with no traffic to disturb them. You see a ring in the water and you say: "That's a trout" and you drop your fly right in the centre. And whoops, he's on your line!'

'Does he fight?'

'Does he not! Dash up and down, you've got to have

skill to land a trout, and it's not easy to keep your feet, for often you are wading and the stones are slippery.'

'How did you learn?'

The bailiff smiled as he remembered.

'To be a good fly fisherman you don't want water – not to start with. All you need is an open space. A bit of lawn's splendid or, if you haven't got that, if you can pick a quiet time there's the park or a recreation ground.'

'What d'you do?'

'You take your rod and you practise. What you want to do is to learn to put your fly down on the water exactly where you want it.'

'In the middle of the circle where you know there's a trout.'

'That's it, son. For practice you don't want a fly on your line, just a bit of rag.' The bailiff stood up and held an imaginary rod. First he held it straight, then, with a flick of his wrist, he shot out his line; when he had finished the rod was nearly vertical and the line, as Andrew could almost see, had flown out to just above where a trout was lying.

Andrew had no idea why but that talk with the bailiff had done something to him. He became obsessed with trout. The very next day he got a book on trout fishing out of the public library. He had shown it to his father.

'Look, Dad. Couldn't we go where we could catch trout?'

His father laughed.

'Not likely! Too expensive and too like hard work. I like to sit for my fishing and watch my float.'

That was when Andrew knew he must keep his fly fishing dreams to himself. And that was when he began borrowing his father's rod. His father's day began very early round about four o'clock when he and Uncle Bob drove off in the van to Covent Garden. Soon afterwards Andrew, holding the rod, crept out of the house. He went to the recreation ground; it was closed but there was a place where he could climb over. There he practised casting, and before the winter came he could throw his imaginary fly pretty near anywhere he wanted inside about twenty feet.

In winter, when there was little chance of line-throwing, Andrew learned to make flies. A library book showed him the different ones and the tools he would need. It also told him to look out for feathers and bits of fur. He kept all these things hidden but that did not mean that there was no sign of his work about.

'I don't know what you do in your bedroom, Andrew,' his mother would grumble. 'There's always bits of feathers and that stuck to your carpet.'

Had she known it there were always four or five flies in an envelope in Andrew's pocket. He knew there was no point in carrying them about but he liked to feel they were there.

The only person who knew what Andrew was doing was Angela. She had to be told because he used to sleep so heavily when he got back to bed after his practice throwing she had to see he woke up. She had to be told too because Andrew's dream of catching a trout grew too big for him to keep to himself and, of course, someone had to admire the flies. Oddly, for someone who didn't like fishing, Angela liked hearing about it.

'Go on,' she would say. 'Tell how he rushes up and down and you nearly fall in the river.' So it wasn't really so peculiar that it was Angela who shared the great adventure.

It was the Whitsun weekend. As usual the family were in Kent. For once the weather was kind. The sun blazed, the woods were blue with bluebells and every bird was singing. But amongst the fishermen there was trouble. The wife of one of them was taken ill, and it was generally agreed it seemed like appendicitis. She didn't want an ambulance and to be taken to hospital, she wanted her own doctor. The children's father and mother talked things over.

'We'd better take the poor soul in the van,' the children's mother said. 'I'll go with you to help.'

'Looks like we did ought,' the children's father agreed. He looked sadly at his rod. 'Take most of the day, shouldn't wonder. I'll let Andrew have a fish, might make him keen again.'

No sooner had the van driven off than Angela came out with her plan.

'At that big house we drive past there's a lake. What say we take the line and you catch a trout?'

'It would be trespassing.'

Angela shook her head.

'Not if you put the trout back it wouldn't. There's a bit of the lake hidden under trees, nobody would see. Anyway, I think the house is empty.'

They thumbed a lift and were dropped off a hundred yards from the house.

'If we go into the field next to the house nobody will see us,' said Angela. 'Come on, and hide the rod.'

They climbed a gate and ran up the side of a field to where an iron fencing enclosed the land round the grounds.

'Get over,' Angela whispered, 'and keep bent until we get to the trees.'

It was a lovely lake. Neither child knew what it meant but across it mayflies were skimming, so of course the trout were rising.

To Andrew it was all he had read about come true.

'Look at those circles, it's trout making them!'

Angela looked round. The trees sheltered them from the house. There was not a soul about.

'Get on with it. Got a fly ready?'

Of course Andrew had a fly, he had even got a mayfly looking not at all unlike what he saw on the water. He unpacked the rod, fixed it together then took the envelope from his pocket. 'Don't buy cheap hooks,' the book had said, so he had bought the best. The mayfly had been fiddly to make, a spider was easier for it had no wings. He looked over his shoulder – he was sufficiently far from the trees to cast his fly safely. There a huge ring was forming. As calmly as if he was practising in the recreation ground he flicked his wrist, the line shot forward. It was beginner's luck: the fly landed dead centre of the ring and was taken.

There isn't anything more exciting than the tug on the line given when a fly is taken. Andrew had only what the book said to guide him how to play his fish.

Angela was carrying their father's keep-net, which was the only net they had.

'Have the net ready,' Andrew gasped. 'I'll tell you when.'

It seemed to Andrew and Angela half an hour at least while the fish thrashed up and down the lake. Remembering what he had read, Andrew let him tire himself while drawing him nearer. At last he shouted – neither of them in the excitement had remembered to keep quiet.

'Got him! Get the net ready.'

It was a beautiful trout. The children gazed at it in ecstasy. Then Andrew said:

'I must take the hook out.'

Angela knelt on the grass by the trout.

'Be as gentle as you can. Don't hurt him.'

Andrew had learned how to extract hooks from his father. As kindly as possible he removed the hook, then, with his eyes shut – for who could watch their first trout thrown back into the water – he let it go. There was a splash, a flash of silver and just an ever-widening ring on the water.

'Do you know you're trespassing?'

The children jumped. Standing beside them was an old gentleman wearing a tweed suit and cap.

'Only sort of,' said Angela. 'We did put him back.'

The old man was staring at Andrew.

'Who taught you to fish, boy?'

Andrew explained. About his father and practising on the recreation ground, and the library book and tying flies.

'I'm terribly sorry, sir. But honestly I don't think he was hurt. He swam away all right.'

'How long have you been practising fly fishing without ever seeing water, let alone a trout?' the old gentleman asked.

Andrew calculated.

'About a year.'

The old gentleman's voice was almost respectful.

'And you catch your first trout – two and a half pounds if an ounce – and you throw him back.'

'I didn't want to,' Andrew confessed. 'But we were trespassing.'

There was a long silence, during which Andrew and Angela saw the police being fetched. Then the old man said:

'My boy caught his first trout when he was ten. How old are you?'

'Eleven.'

'It wasn't as big as yours. But I had it mounted and put in a case. It's still in his room.'

'I expect he's caught lots since,' said Angela.

'Oh, he did, but not now. He was an airman in the war, he didn't come back.'

Andrew could think of nothing to say to that. Angela said:

'I'm glad he had his first fish to keep.'

The old man seemed to come to a decision.

'I'll get out the car and drive you back. I'd like a word with your father.'

'Oh, must you!' said Andrew. 'He'll be awfully angry

about the trespassing, and he doesn't understand about trout.'

The old man laid a hand on Andrew's shoulder.

'To trespass was wrong, but putting back the trout was the action of a hero. I'm going to arrange with your father to let you visit me. This lake has been waiting for another young fisherman.'

The Old Fool

How Aunt Henrietta came by The Old Fool was a mystery. That he came by some sort of accident was the only method of accounting for him for he was not an endearing dog, not the sort anyone would buy, besides, up to his arrival Aunt Henrietta had hated dogs, even the sort that everybody else simply had to pat. He was a whitish Pekinese of exceptionally doubtful pedigree, rather heavy in build, rather short of breath, and suffering from a mild skin trouble. The skin trouble kept him endlessly scratching, and as he scratched he complained to himself in a low whine. Aunt Henrietta called him

Snuggles; no one blamed the wretched dog for that but decently ignored it, calling him before his mistress 'Hi you' and behind her back 'The Old Fool'.

For ten days in August each year Aunt Henrietta visited her nephew John and his family.

John and Lucille had three pekes, Ping, Pong and Poo, and three children, Tony, Lavinia and Bill. The pekes were very royal gentlemen, so pure of their breeding that they could afford to ignore it. Left to themselves they would have tolerated The Old Fool, though they were unused to meeting dogs of his class. Aunt Henrietta, however, had felt it was so nice for all the dear little dogs to be friends that she had tried to promote it by rubbing The Old Fool's nose against theirs, saying 'Kissy, kissy'. Unjustly, Ping, Pong and Poo had failed to notice that The Old Fool disliked this as much as they did. It was difficult to say which of them bit him, but bitten he was. It was only the first of many bites given not so much in ill will as to show unwillingness for forced friendships.

Tony and Lavinia, the older children, were fond of most dogs, but they had clear ideas as to what they should be like, and The Old Fool fell far short. It was impossible for either Tony or Lavinia to see anything so in need of reformation and not to do what they could. They tried to thin him, to make him interested in the right things, they gave him drastic cures for whatever made him scratch. Their well-meant efforts resulted in trouble, row after row throughout the ten days Aunt Henrietta was in the house, so when he came the following year they had lost interest.

The third year, Aunt Henrietta broke her leg and while she was recuperating in a nursing home, The Old Fool became a more or less permanent guest for the duration of her recovery. Bill had been only two when first The Old Fool had come to the house, and he had scarcely seen him for he was always being reformed by Tony and Lavinia. It was the next year when he was three, nearly four, and The Old Fool had begun to be ignored, that they became acquainted. It was a quiet little friendship unstressed by either of them, for both knew he was a dog with whom friendship was considered beneath one's dignity. If they were about together it was an accident. But in the third summer, when he was rising five, Bill found his heart suddenly swelling when he saw The Old Fool arrive, and then he knew he loved him.

When your brother is nine and going to a proper school next term, and your sister will soon be eight, it's natural they won't bother much with a person who isn't even five. Besides, all the things they did never seemed to want three. They had all sorts of games down by the river and this year a boat. Bill had been out in the boat so he knew how nice it was. So when he saw Tony and Lavinia starting out with Ping, Pong and Poo, he would drop whatever he was doing and start off hopefully beside them. They were always kind. 'You stay here, Bill darling,' Lavinia would say, 'you wouldn't like what we're going to do.' So Bill stayed, and went on playing, humming a bit to keep his spirits up because it's not nice being left behind even if you don't like the things other people are going to do. Then The Old Fool would come along, and while Bill hummed he would scratch and whine, and between them they made nice companionable sounds.

When Aunt Henrietta broke her leg Bill was most concerned for The Old Fool. Aunt Henrietta might not be everybody's idea of a friend, but she was fond of him and with her in a nursing home there didn't seem many friends left. Bill hoped The Old Fool hadn't noticed that the others didn't like him much, but he was afraid he must. It was not that he didn't get his rights but somehow he was satisfied with less than other people. His dinner was exactly the same as the other dogs', Bill looked every day to make sure, and it was served on the same sort of plate, but he was always swindled out of the last mouthfuls. 'Swallow yours down, boys,' Pong would whisper to Ping and Poo, and then after some rapid gulping they would swing round and clear everything left on The Old Fool's plate. His basket was better if anything than the other dogs' baskets, for his had a pink bow and pink blanket, but Pong's went on John's floor, and Ping's by Lavinia's bed, and Poo's by Tony's, and The Old Fool's went into the boot-room after Aunt Henrietta went into the nursing home. The boot-room was dry and quite nice but Bill felt that somehow it wasn't fair.

Bill sat at the end of the table at meals, next to John, and the dogs had their dinners under the window beside him, so he knew just how often The Old Fool was jostled out of his rights. When he could, he put things in his pocket to give him afterwards to make up. Meat was difficult because it made a mess, and he was watched to see he ate all that was put on his plate, even the fat, but sometimes ham from breakfast, and bits of bread and lumps of sugar. It was by these tit-bits that The Old Fool's affection for Bill was noticed, for sometimes he would forget himself and loll in a reminding way against his chair. One day when he did this John said:

'The Old Fool will miss you, Bill, when Aunt Henrietta's leg is well, and he goes away.'

Bill turned very red like somebody who is going to

choke. It was the first time he had remembered that The Old Fool would go away again, he had been there so long.

Ping, Pong and Poo disapproved of the friendship between Bill and The Old Fool. The love of the family, even of its smallest members, was their right and not to be grabbed by the passing guest.

'Sucking up to Bill,' Pong said nastily.

The Old Fool saved himself answering by seeming busy scratching.

'You should keep away from him with that nasty skin trouble of yours,' Ping put in. 'He might catch it.'

Poo looked at The Old Fool witheringly.

'Leave him alone, the Aunt's leg will soon be well, and then Bill will forget him.'

Their dinner arrived and The Old Fool stopped scratching to eat, but Ping, Pong and Poo had not done with him.

'Don't wait to finish,' Pong whispered to the other two. 'Dash across and snatch a bit of his. They' – he looked up at the family round the table – 'won't notice.'

But Bill did notice and the injustice made him cry out.

'Those three' – he pointed furiously with his fork at Ping, Pong and Poo – 'have eaten The Old Fool's dinner.'

Hearing the cry, the three dogs hurried back to their own plates. John looked round.

'Rubbish, old man, he's tucking in all right. Anyway, he's too fat.'

Ping, Pong and Poo raised their heads from their plates. They looked at The Old Fool.

'Hear that?'

'You're too fat.'

'It's a kindness to make you diet.'

Just before Tony went to school there was a gymkhana. It was miles away and meant trouble in getting the ponies over, but it was chosen as a last treat, so it was decided to manage it. It meant a long day, starting early and getting back late, and since cars made Bill sick when he was tired, he was told he would have to stay at home. Bill always missed the most important parts of conversations so he only heard that there was a gymkhana and not that he wasn't going. He had ridden in a gymkhana once and got a second prize so he never thought of being left behind; after all he was quite a gymkhana man. When the day came he was so certain that he was included in the arrangements that he insisted on coming down to breakfast in his jodhpurs. Lucille looked worried when she saw them and threw a danger signal round the table. Tony and Lavinia were not interested in danger glances.

'Why have you got those things on?' Tony asked him. 'You know the ponies have gone to the gymkhana.'

Bill turned very red; he looked at John.

'I are going too?'

'No, old boy.' John's voice was almost cross, he hated to hurt him. 'But I'll tell you where you are going, and that's to the shops to spend this.' He laid a half-crown on the table.

Bill watched the family and Ping, Pong and Poo drive away. It was not nice, his world looked very black; he began to hum to keep his spirits up. The Old Fool, sitting near, encouraged by the sound, scratched and whined. It was a nice mixture of noises they made, the day seemed brighter, and then Bill felt the half-crown in his pocket and suddenly things weren't bad at all. He went into the house to find out who was taking him to the shops.

The toy shop was full of everything Bill wanted. After the first twenty minutes spent in choosing a large car he could drive himself, a rocking-horse with a face just like one of the ponies, and a train that really went on proper lines with signal boxes and all, and finding they cost more than half a crown, the tactful saleswoman led him to a corner where the goods were suited to the thinner purse. The things there Bill found were just as good, though smaller, and if they went it was by winding a key and not by themselves like the train. It took a long time to select among a vast amount of treasures, but in the end he found something he knew he could not live without. It was a boat. Not just a little flimsy boat but a solid thing cut out of a nice chunk of wood and looking very like the punt John had given Tony and Lavinia. Once he had found it he never thought of not being able to have it, and he was quite right, it cost the money he had, a whole half-crown.

Back at the house, he showed the boat to everybody and was told that after tea he should go down to the river and float it.

'Launch it,' said Bill reprovingly. He knew things about boats.

He sat down on the bank in front of the house and showed the boat to The Old Fool, and tried to make it look as though it was floating on the lawn. There is nothing more aggravating than a new boat without the water to try it in. Bill did not exactly mean to do anything wrong, but presently he found himself running down the path to the river with The Old Fool puffing behind.

What goes on in the heads of the designers, owners and builders of great ships at the moment of their launching is uncertain, but it is certain that none of them are more anxious than was Bill as he launched his boat on the river. She proved to be a masterpiece of design. She sat squarely on the river as if she had been born there and slid gently forward with the wind-driven water as though she had travelled far seas all her days. She did not travel fast, there was not enough water for that, but she kept Bill and The Old Fool busy running beside her – and then a tragedy occurred. A snag caught her, she turned off her course and moved out into the middle of the stream. Bill did all the things that are right in such emergencies. He threw large stones behind her that their ripples might carry her in, and he took a stick and made a terrific storm in the water hoping that it would be a storm the right way; it wasn't, it was the wrong way and carried the boat further out. Then he found a really long stick and, running down the bank, he waited at a place where there was a nice little branch to hold on to and leaned forward to try and catch her. The stick seemed just long enough; leaning forward as far as he could he felt it touch her, and then suddenly there was a loose feeling, the branch behind him gave way, and Bill shot into the water.

It would not have mattered, except for his clothes, if Bill had fallen in just there, because the river was low, and he could have scrambled out, but in his fall he hit his head on a stone. The Old Fool had been having half an eye on the ship launching and half on a rabbit, but seeing there had been an accident he came to the water's edge to investigate. He barked to Bill who made no sign, and his boat, which The Old Fool realised was somehow important, went floating off down the river. The Old Fool loathed water but there are moments when a dog must stifle his dislike, so he gingerly stepped into it. At once he found he had made a mistake, the rocks were deceptive, it was necessary to swim. A little footwork brought him to Bill and he gave a pull at his shirt. It was when Bill made no answer to this that he realised something was wrong. Bill wasn't one to keep still. The Old Fool left him and paddled back to the shore; the water had irritated his skin trouble. He sat down to have a good think and to scratch, and as usual as he scratched he whined, and the more he thought how strange it was that Bill should lie so still, the more he whined until finally his whines became howls.

The water bailiff, about on his duties, was a quarter

of a mile up the river when The Old Fool's howls began. He stopped and listened.

'Dang me if that dog isn't in trouble.' He ran.

John and Lucille were fetched back by telephone. No one could bring Bill round, no one knew how long his face had been in the water except The Old Fool, and he couldn't talk. Two hours the doctor worked and had almost given up hope when suddenly way down in Bill's subconscious there stirred a wish to come home from the land to which he had floated, there were nice things he did not want to miss, perhaps he knew that his mum and dad had just arrived and that his mum was crying, and perhaps he thought of The Old Fool. Anyway he opened his eyes.

Bill's birthday was an important sort of day for not only was it his birthday, but The Old Fool was his very own. Aunt Henrietta, mellowed perhaps by hours of meditation in bed, was moved by what had happened and wrote to wish him a happy birthday and to make a present of darling Snuggles. Then before lunch a very grand thing happened. His father said:

'Here, Bill old man, fix this to The Old Fool's collar.' And he held out a silver medal. It was a lovely medal with a picture of The Old Fool on one side and 'For saving Bill's life' in big letters on the other.

Bill was awed.

'A medal for him? Like what soldiers have.'

He knelt down by The Old Fool and his mother helped him to fix it to his collar. She was slow at helping because her eyes were full of tears.

Ping, Pong and Poo looked at the medal.

'That's nothing,' they said loudly. 'Anybody can bark.'

But when Pong saw Ping and Poo making a move he growled:

'Get back. Give The Old Fool a chance.'

Let's Go Coaching

The Garlands lived in a part of London called Pimlico. They were a family of four. Mr Garland was a schoolmaster. Mrs Garland was just a mum but an especially gorgeous sort of one. Angus was seven and Prue, which was short for Prudence, was six.

Angus and Prudence went to the same school, which was not far from the Victoria Coach Station. Sometimes, when there wasn't too much shopping, the children would ask their mother if they could go home past the coach station.

'Please, Mum,' Angus would say. 'Could today be a coach station day?'

Then Prue, jumping about, would join in.

'Oh, please, Mum! Please!'

When the answer was 'yes' often their mother would add:

'Though what you two are so fond of the coach station for beats me. Give me a nice railway station.'

Outside the coach station Angus always tried to see how many coaches he could spot going to the furthest away places. What Prue liked doing was looking at the families and their luggage. She guessed where they were off to and why.

'Look, Mum, I think they're going miles and miles and it'll be by the sea. That little boy has got a toy boat.'

Then, Angus, who had been spelling out a word, would interrupt.

'My goodness, that coach in the corner says "Aberdeen". Imagine anyone going as far as Aberdeen!'

Then one day the coach station stopped being a place from which other people travelled. Instead it became the place from which the Garlands travelled.

It was all because of Aunt Hattie's wedding. Aunt Hattie was Dad's youngest sister. The children had known for a long time that one day she was going to marry a doctor. Suddenly plans were changed because the doctor was going abroad, so the wedding was six weeks away.

'I'm afraid it will be an awful rush,' Aunt Hattie wrote, 'but please I want Angus to carry my train and Prue to be a bridesmaid.'

Prue was thrilled. Her friend Alice had been a bridesmaid so she knew it meant a beautiful new frock.

'Will I wear pink right down to the ground with flowers in my hair like Alice did?'

'Girls!' growled Angus. 'Imagine wanting to wear flowers in your hair! You'll look terrible.'

Dad smiled at Prue.

'I think she'll look pretty good myself. What I'm worrying about is how you'll look as a page, Angus.'

Prue got her own back.

'You certainly aren't the sort of boy to look his best in blue satin. That's what the pages wore when Alice was a bridesmaid.'

'Blue satin!' Angus was appalled. 'Mum, Aunt Hattie doesn't think I'll wear blue satin, does she, because I absolutely won't.'

Mum had finished reading the letter.

'How you children do go on. No, Angus, you are

wearing a kilt. Somebody is lending the whole outfit, thank goodness.'

Prue was bouncing up and down.

'And me, Mum? Is it pink right down to the ground?'

Mum looked in the envelope and took out a piece of paper with a picture drawn on it.

'Not pink, I'm afraid. But very pretty. A sort of gold colour. Look.'

Prue took the piece of paper. On it was a drawing of a little girl who looked rather like she did. She was wearing a dress with a tight bodice and a full skirt all the way to the floor. On her head was a sort of small crown of flowers. She was carrying a little bouquet. To the paper was pinned a piece of gold-coloured silk.

Prue could hardly speak.

'Imagine me looking like that child does!'

Mum could see very well how Prue would look. She was so fair she would look quite lovely in gold. But all she said was:

'That dress is going to take quite a lot of making. They are posting the material from Liverpool. I hope it comes today.'

'Talking of Liverpool,' Dad said, 'do you think you could find time to go to the coach station today and find out what time the coaches go? We ought to book right away. They get so full in the summer.'

A wedding and a coach journey too! Some things are too exciting to bear unless you move about. All in a moment Angus and Prue were dancing round the living room, jumping over chairs shouting: 'A coach and a wedding! A coach and a wedding!'

After school that afternoon Mum took the children to the coach station. There were crowds of people outside and inside. The outside ones were getting out of taxis or struggling along carrying suitcases. The inside ones were doing different things. Some were queueing with their luggage to get on to the coaches. Some were already sitting on the coaches. Some were sitting on benches looking as if they might go on sitting on them for weeks. Some – and there were a lot of these – were in the restaurant eating and drinking.

Angus looked round.

'I wonder where our coach will start from.'

It was gorgeous to say 'our coach', it made the children feel as if they were going to Liverpool that very minute.

They looked round. The names of the places the coaches were going to were hanging from the roof. White lines on the ground made parking places for each group of coaches. But they couldn't see Liverpool anywhere. There were lots of men in uniform walking about so Mum stopped one.

'Please could you tell me where the Liverpool coaches start from?'

The man was very nice and helpful. He pointed to the right.

'Over there. Are you going on tonight's coach?'

'No,' Mum explained. 'We are only looking today, but we wanted to know where our coach does start from when the time comes.'

'Of course,' the man agreed. Then he smiled at the children. 'You let us know when you're travelling and we'll give your coach a special wash and polish.'

'I know he was teasing,' said Angus, 'but it was a friendly thing to say.'

They went to the enquiry counter. There a lady gave them a paper about coaches to Liverpool. Mum led the way to a seat and they sat down while she read it. Presently she said:

'We can go to Liverpool up the big new motorways. Or we can go through lovely places like Oxford and Stratford-on-Avon, or we can travel all night. Now, I wonder what way your dad will like us to go. I think we had better go home and see him.'

It seemed ages before Dad came home to tea. When

he did both Angus and Prue talked at once. As a result it was quite a long time before he knew what they were saying. Then he said to Mum:

'Let's have a look at the timetable they gave you. Oh, my word, listen to the names of the places our coach goes to! They sound as gay as beads on a string. Loudwater. The Pig and Whistle, Postcombe. Oxford. Woodstock. Chapel House for Chipping Norton. Stratford-on-Avon. Warwick. Kenilworth. Chester. It reads like a history book.'

'I daresay,' said Mum. 'But the question is how do we book? It's much quicker to travel by the motorway.'

'Quicker!' Dad sniffed. 'Who wants to be quick when one can catch a glimpse of such exciting places? What do you say, children?'

Actually Angus and Prue hadn't felt too keen when Dad said the timetable read like a history book. Would he give them a history lesson all the way? But he sounded so excited it made them excited too.

'Who wants to be quick?' they agreed.

'I tell you what though,' Dad suggested. 'How about seeing everything on the road up. Then coming back home we could travel on the night coach. We shan't want to see so much then for we'll be tired after the wedding.'

The next day after school Mum and the two children

went back to the coach station. This time they walked in looking as if it was something they did every day. They went right through the station. Past crowds of people getting on to coaches going to the south coast. Through the enquiry hall. Then round a corner and there was the ticket office.

'Two whole and two halves to Liverpool on the twelfth of next month,' said Mum.

Time is very odd. When something gorgeous is going to happen it crawls. When it's something beastly it rushes. Look how slow time is between one birthday and another. Or how it creeps as December passes when everybody is waiting for Christmas Day. But if it is something horrid, even if it starts by being weeks away, in a flash it's happening tomorrow.

For Angus and Prue it took so long to get to the twelfth, sometimes they despaired it would ever come. It was a little better for Prue than it was for Angus for she could at least watch her bridesmaid's frock being made. She tried to make Angus take an interest.

'Mum says I look like a princess in a fairy story, and that's without my crown of flowers.'

Angus could not care less what Prue was going to look like. That he had to dress up, even in a kilt, was the one thing he didn't like about going to Liverpool.

'Will you stop going on about that bridesmaid's dress. I'll see it on the wedding day, won't I?'

At last it was next month. Then the days crept by. Then it was the tenth. Then it was the eleventh. MUM WAS PACKING. Then it was the twelfth.

'Oh, frabjous day!' said Angus when he woke up.

'It's coach day! It's coach day! It's coach day!' sang Prue.

'You must all eat a good breakfast,' Mum said. 'We don't stop for elevenses until after twelve.'

It's not easy to eat when you feel full up with excitement. But somehow everybody did eat: first a plate of cereal, then a boiled egg with plenty of bread and butter. The children drank milk and Mum and Dad lots of tea.

They went by taxi to the coach station. Actually they started in lots of time but the children were scared they would be late.

'What would we do if, just as we got there, we saw our coach leaving?' Angus asked Dad.

Dad looked at his watch.

'It won't leave for twenty minutes. But if it had left we'd take the taxi on to the first stop.'

'Stop fussing,' said Mum. 'Dad wouldn't let us miss it. You know that.'

Of course the coach hadn't gone. It was waiting just where they had been told by the nice man in uniform that it would be. The driver was standing behind it putting the customers' luggage into the boot. They had two suitcases and he took them from Dad.

'Liverpool. OK, sir.'

Then they climbed into the coach. Dad and Mum shared one seat. Angus and Prue sat in front of them on another. Soon the coach filled up. Then the driver came in. When he had checked everybody's tickets he climbed into his seat. Then, with a roar, the engine started up: they were off. Dad said:

'If we had been doing this journey a hundred and fifty years ago we wouldn't be in a motor coach. We'd have been pulled by horses. Rather as you see them in those Westerns on TV.'

It was quite a thought. At once both Angus and Prue were imagining themselves in a stage coach.

'How many horses would we have?' Angus wondered.

'Usually it was four,' said Dad. 'There weren't all these passengers in those days. Only six inside, the rest had to travel outside. That must have been miserable in the winter or on wet days.'

'And they wouldn't get there on the same day like we are going to,' Mum pointed out. 'It took days, didn't it?'

Dad nodded.

'At best horses only managed five miles an hour, whereas we'll be doing well over sixty on a good road.'

Angus looked out of the window. They were passing through the outskirts of London. The road was full of traffic. There were honking cars, bicycles, both motorbikes and the pedal sort, every type of commercial vehicle and, of course, buses.

'What would have been on the road a hundred and fifty years ago?'

'Private coaches,' said Dad. 'Rich people had those. Carts. People on horseback.'

Prue too had been thinking.

'I wonder if people like us went to weddings on a stage coach.'

'With a gold frock amongst the luggage,' Mum reminded her. 'If such a little girl did travel I expect she hoped very hard the coach would not be held up by highwaymen.'

Prue had forgotten about highwaymen.

'Ooh! But they don't steal frocks, do they?'

Dad patted Prue's shoulder.

'Whatever else we meet on the road it won't be a highwayman.'

They stopped at a village called Stokenchurch for

elevenses. Angus and Prue had Coke and buns. Dad and Mum had sandwiches and coffee. Then they were off again for Stratford-on-Avon, where they were to have lunch.

Perhaps it was that they ate a lot of lunch. Or it was because both Angus and Prue were still thinking about the days of stage coaches. Four horses make the drowsiest clip-clop noise. But after Stratford-on-Avon something made them fall asleep. They must have slept a long time for when they woke up the coach had stopped again. This time the place was called Prees Heath.

At Prees Heath it was too late for tea so the children had sandwiches, ice creams and another Coke. Mum and Dad had sandwiches and a drink.

'This is our last stop,' said Mum. 'In less than two hours we shall be in Liverpool where Grandfather will meet us.'

This time it was Dad and Mum who fell asleep. Angus and Prue were too busy counting the places the coach passed through. Angus spelled out as many names as he could. Whitchurch. Hampton Cross Roads. Broxton Chester. Ellesmere Port. Little Sutton. Bromborough Cross. Rock Ferry. It was there the terrifying thing happened. They had stopped to let some passengers off. Before the coach could start again two real live

highwaymen leapt on to it. They wore black masks and
each held a pistol. Both shouted: 'Your money or your
life.'

Prue tried to scream but she was so scared nothing
came out but a faint bleat. Angus was very brave.

'I shan't give them anything. I've only got my shilling
to spend in Liverpool and they aren't having that.'

'Oh Angus!' Prue whispered. 'You must give it them.
They'll kill you if you don't. Oh dear, will they take my
frock?'

'Of course not, it's money and jewels highwaymen like.'

'Dad said we couldn't meet a highwayman.'

Angus clutched his shilling in his pocket.

'How wrong can he be?'

The highwaymen were coming down the coach. One on the right side, the other on the left. The children could hear the clink of money and, they supposed, jewels.

'Oh dear!' Prue moaned. 'It's almost us.'

But when their highwayman reached them he did not look as fierce as he had at a distance. So Angus dared to speak.

'Are you a real, true highwayman?'

The highwayman lifted the mask which was over his eyes. Then he winked.

'Today I am but as a rule I'm a hospital student.'

Dad and Mum had woken up. Dad held out some money.

'Will this spare our lives?'

So they weren't after all real highwaymen. Just hospital students raising money for their hospitals. Prue was glad but Angus had a feeling he had been cheated. It would have been much more exciting if it had been a real hold-up.

Then it was Liverpool. Grandfather, smiling like the Cheshire cat, was waiting. The great journey was over.

'But only one way,' Angus said to Prue. 'The day after tomorrow we'll do it again the other way round.'

Prue's eyes sparkled like stars.

'And that time we'll travel all through the night and I'll have been a bridesmaid.'

Howard

It started as an ordinary morning in the rectory. The rector, his wife Rose and their three children eating breakfast. The rector dividing his interest between food and *The Times*. Rose absentmindedly pouring out and passing food while she read the account of the Women's Institute outing in the local paper. The three children – Paul aged thirteen, Emma twelve and Patrick ten – eating without pause while each talked about their own doings without minding that no one was listening.

Then the post came. Patrick fetched it. It was mostly for the rector but there were two for Rose. Regretfully the rector laid aside *The Times*, for the coming of the post was to him the sign that the working day had begun. Paul, who had waited for this moment, grabbed *The Times* and turned to the cricket news.

There was never any secret about Rose's letters for, as she opened them, she kept up a running commentary. That morning she said: 'This is from that Mrs Ripley who has come to live at the Red House. Oh dear, I had hopes of using her at the fête but she's going to Spain. Why should anyone want to go to Spain the moment they have moved in?' She turned to the other letter. 'This is from Grundy. I do hope it's not to say his rheumatism is bad again. I had counted on having him for an hour or two so the garden will be looking its best for the fête.'

It was at that moment that the rector laid down the letter he was reading.

'My dear,' he said to Rose, 'Gena wants Howard to come and stay with us.'

The three children stared at their father. Emma spoke first.

'The revolting Howard? Why?'

Patrick piled some more honey on his toast.

'He'll simply hate it here.'

Paul faced his father.

'I don't think if you let Howard come it's strictly fair, do you?'

Money being scarce in the rectory it was accepted by the children that the parents took their holiday while they were away at their boarding schools, for obviously an away-holiday for two cost far less than an away-holiday for five. But in return, though it had never been explicitly stated, the children expected that their holiday at home should be spent in such ways as they preferred to spend them with the least possible parental interference, and no engagements forced on them which they might dislike. Clearly Howard, not just coming for a meal, which would be bad enough, but actually staying in the house, was a shocking breach of the understanding.

The rector accepted Paul's reproof.

'Too true, I'm sure it's grossly unfair to land Howard on you but I don't see how I can get out of it.'

'Why can't you, dear?' Rose asked. 'Gena ignores us for years and then calmly asks us to have Howard to stay. Why should we?'

The rector sighed, for he could see his family would gang up against him.

'Well, he is my only brother's child.'

'He's always been that,' Paul pointed out, 'and when

Uncle Peter was first killed in that air smash you never stopped asking if Howard could come and stay.'

'You even asked Aunt Gena too though you always hated her,' Emma reminded her father.

The rector looked stern.

'That's nonsense! I never hated your Aunt Gena or anybody else. I may have found her rather difficult to get on with – no more.'

The children exchanged looks. Of course their father hadn't hated Aunt Gena for it was true he hated nobody but tried to love everybody. All the same it was family knowledge that Uncle Peter's marriage to Aunt Gena had from the beginning been considered a disaster, for she was, according to those who had met her, abysmally silly and very conceited. Still, when Uncle Peter was killed, their father and the grandparents had fallen over themselves trying to help, but had not been allowed to. In fact there had not been much time to help, for six months after Uncle Peter's death Aunt Gena had married again. This time to a theatrical agent.

It was the theatrical agent who had spotted the possibilities in his stepson. Howard was at that time a good-looking, fair-haired seven-year-old, just what was wanted for a star role in a film. Howard had never looked back. He had contracts in Hollywood and in

England and, now that he was twelve and old enough to appear in person, he was to star in his own BBC TV series, which was to be shown on both sides of the Atlantic.

'Why does Gena want us to have him?' Rose asked. 'It'll be very dull for him here.'

The rector read what Gena had written out loud:

'"The doctor says that darling Howard"' – the children made rude noises – '"needs a complete change with other children. Unkind man, he won't even let his mummy go on holiday with him."'

'Oh dear,' said Rose, 'Gena doesn't sound as if she has changed, does she?'

Paul shook his head at his father.

'Quite truthfully, Dad, you know it won't do. We don't want the loathsome Howard here. He's a spoilt brat and he'll muck up the holidays for all of us. You can't give one good reason why we should put up with him.'

The rector had an answer ready.

'Oh yes, I can. Death watch beetles. As you all know, we have them in the church. The repairs are going to cost a fortune. At this moment I don't know where the money is coming from.'

'The church fête,' said Patrick.

'The church fête will help, we hope,' his father agreed,

'but to make real money we want a church fête to which people will come from all over the county. Until I got this letter I had thought that impossible but now I see a ray of light.'

Emma caught the idea.

'You mean advertise that Howard will be there?'

The rector nodded.

'Not only there, he can open it.'

The children looked disgusted.

'Really, Dad!' Paul expostulated. 'Fancy you sinking so low!'

The rector did not look ashamed.

'When you have death watch beetles you have to take any help you can snatch.'

Emma made a face.

'Imagine Howard prancing around making speeches and signing autographs! Having him will be ghastly enough without that.'

Rose was coming round to the idea of Howard as she accepted any idea that would help her husband.

'You've never seen Howard. He may be a nice boy.'

'Nice!' said Emma. 'A girl at school had an article about him in a magazine which she lent me to read. He sounded hopeless.'

The rector's eyes twinkled.

'From the sound of it I am not the only one to cash in on Howard. I doubt if the girl who showed you the article would have known Howard was your cousin if you hadn't told her.'

'Touché!' said Paul. 'I suppose we've all cashed in on the little beast being a relation – it has a sort of snob value.'

'Quite,' his father agreed. 'That's why I am expecting him to lure the whole county to the fête. If anyone will attract enough money to oust the death watch beetles it will be Howard.'

Since it was no good fighting against Howard coming to stay the children made plans to ensure he spoilt the holidays as little as possible.

'If Dad wants him to draw the whole county to the fête we can't let people see him beforehand, so we'll have to keep him out of sight,' Paul pointed out, 'which means we can't enter him for the tennis.'

One of the features of the summer holidays was a knock-out tennis tournament for all ages.

'Anyway I don't suppose he plays tennis,' said Emma. 'I don't suppose he does any ordinary things.'

Patrick spoke with envy.

'He rides. I saw him in a film.'

Emma tried to sound knowledgeable.

'That doesn't mean he can ride, it could be some-body called a double riding for him. I expect they'd be afraid to let him ride a horse in case he fell off and got hurt.'

There were no ponies at the rectory, but ponies could be hired when funds allowed, and entered for competitions at the gymkhana held at the end of the summer holidays. It was up to each child to decide how funds allotted for the holidays should be spent. To date they had never made the gymkhana, so many other things had eaten away the holiday money. It was tough to think that Howard might enter, but it had to be considered.

'If he's staying that long,' said Paul gloomily, 'I sup-pose we'll have to tell him about the gymkhana, it'll be pretty maddening if he enters and we can only go and watch.'

Two days later the children were given a new view of Howard's visit.

'I've had another letter from your Aunt Gena,' their father told them. 'It seems Howard is a very rich young man and he is paying us handsomely to stay here. Your mother and I have decided to spend that money on you children, so you can plan a good time for yourselves and Howard.'

'Gosh!' exclaimed Patrick. 'Do you mean we can all enter for the gymkhana?'

'Yes, and hire ponies for treks,' his mother agreed.

'And you can hire that dinghy all the time he's here,' their father added.

'It's tragic,' said Emma, 'that when good fortune strikes this family it has to come in such a hateful way.'

Her father was not having that.

'That's very uncharitable. It's not right to judge the poor boy before you've even seen him.'

Paul came to his sister's rescue.

'Talking of which, when are we to see him?'

His father opened the letter he had received that morning and read:

'"Howard is seeing us off at the airport on Wednesday and then the chauffeur will drive him down to you. He says he should be at the rectory by tea time. I would suggest Howard keep the chauffeur and the Rolls, but as he will want the car after the holidays when his TV series starts I think it is better the chauffeur has his holiday now. Please hire cars when necessary. Howard never travels by public transport in case he is mobbed by fans ... "' The rector folded the letter and put it back in its envelope. 'I have not told your Aunt Gena about the fête – very dishonest of me, I am afraid, but I had to consider the death watch beetles.'

On the Wednesday at four o'clock a chauffeur-driven Rolls-Royce drove in at the rectory gates and out stepped Howard. His face was almost as well known as Prince Charles's. He had hair so fair it was nearly white. It fell across his forehead in what the film papers called 'a Howard wave'. He was small for his age and thin, almost skinny. He was very pale, and had enormous brown eyes with lashes that should have belonged to a girl. He was dressed in a neat blue suit and in every way looked like a creature from another world beside the tough,

brown-haired, brown-skinned rectory children, dressed in faded jeans. Rose was touched by his appearance. 'Poor scrap,' she thought, 'we must feed him up and get him in the sun, he looks terribly pale.' Out loud she said:

'Hullo, Howard! It's lovely to see you.'

The chauffeur had unloaded Howard's luggage. Three beautiful matching cases in blue leather.

'I'll carry these in and then I'll get going. I want to get back to London tonight.'

Rose showed the chauffeur the way to the spare bedroom in which Howard was to sleep. As they climbed the stairs the chauffeur whispered:

'He won't tell you, but he's been very sick on the way down. So don't worry if he doesn't fancy his tea.'

'Poor boy! Is he often carsick?'

'Always on a long journey. He's all right if he sits in front with me but his mother doesn't allow it . . . '

Rose gave the chauffeur a friendly grin, for Howard had been sitting in the front when the car arrived.

'I'll give him something to put him right. Don't worry, we'll take care of him.'

The chauffeur nodded.

'I can see that. This'll be the best break Howard ever had, I shouldn't wonder.'

But looking after Howard and seeing he had a good

time proved much more difficult than the family had imagined, and in a totally different way. For Howard was not grand or stuck up, in fact he seemed if anything cowed. There appeared to be no power to enjoy anything in him. To everything suggested he replied politely: 'Thank you. That will be very nice,' or 'Thank you, I am sure I shall enjoy that.'

By the end of the first week of his visit the family were in despair.

'Almost he'd be better if he was awful in the way we expected,' Emma told her mother. 'I don't think he enjoys anything. We let him ride Robin, who is much the best of the ponies in the stables, but he never even gave him a pat. And when we take him sailing he just sits, he doesn't want to help sail, and I don't think he took in we were playing in the tennis.'

'He spoils everything,' Paul grumbled. 'It's awful carting somebody about who looks as if he is doing whatever we do as a duty.'

Patrick stammered with indignation.

'Imagine being a film star and creeping about as if you were less than nobody!'

It was the next day that the rector at luncheon broke the news to Howard that he was to open the fête. He told him quite casually for he had accepted the belief that

Howard did not care what happened to him. But news of the fête brought Howard to life. He gripped the table so hard his knuckles were white and his face turned even paler than it was normally, and there were tears in his eyes.

'Oh no! Oh, please no!'

The family were amazed.

'Why don't you want to?' Patrick asked. 'It's a piece of cake, the sort of thing you do every day.'

'Anyway it's too late to make a fuss,' Emma pointed out, 'the posters are printed.'

'Dad's having trouble with death watch beetles in the church,' Paul explained. 'He's hoping with you as a draw half the county will pay to come in.'

They might not have spoken for Howard went on looking desperate and refused to finish his lunch.

'It's not that I don't want to help,' he explained, 'it's just I can't, I'll be no good.'

The rector was amazed at such humility.

'Nonsense, you'll be splendid!'

The children were each secretly surprised to find themselves on Howard's side. Poor beast, he might be silent and unenthusiastic but he certainly was not conceited, and if he really did not want to open the fête it seemed mean to make him.

After lunch the rector took Howard to his study to

show him the posters, so the children were alone clearing the table.

'I can't see why he minds,' Paul said, 'but obviously he does, I mean he wasn't putting it on.'

'I vote we ask him,' Patrick suggested. 'If there really is a reason we could tell Dad. I mean, even for the death watch beetles he wouldn't make Howard do it if he really minded.'

Emma doubted that.

'I don't know, those wretched beetles are very close to his heart.'

There was a nice breeze that afternoon so they took Howard out in the sailing dinghy, which his money had hired for them. Not that Howard would enjoy sailing, he never did, and now he knew about the fête he looked paler and limper and less interested even than usual. Paul opened the subject.

'Why do you mind opening the fête, Howard?'

Howard turned so green it looked as if he might be sick. Several times he licked his lips before he managed to answer.

'You wouldn't understand. I mean people like you couldn't.'

'How do you mean, people like us?' Emma asked.

Howard's voice was so low they had to strain to hear him.

'Ordinary people. I mean, none of you are afraid of anything. You are just born brave.'

Patrick was astounded.

'Us brave! We've nothing to be brave about, not like you. I'd be scared stiff if I had to act in a film.'

Howard again licked his lips, they could see he was trying to force himself to say something. At last he got it out.

'I am afraid. You've no idea how awful it is. You see, I'm slipping, everybody knows it.'

'Slipping? Slipping where?' Emma asked.

'From being a star. I haven't the following I had. This TV stunt is a last try, if it doesn't come off I'm washed up.'

He sounded so tragic all three children tried to understand.

'But if you are afraid when you are acting why would you mind giving it up?' Paul asked.

Howard shivered as if suddenly it was winter.

'Mummy would mind. She's sacrificed everything for me. And my stepfather would mind terribly, he's worked like a slave to build me up.'

The children gaped at Howard. This was not in the least the story they had heard. They had heard Aunt Gena and Howard's stepfather lived in luxury on Howard's earnings.

'Would you mind inside yourself if you had to give it up?' Emma asked. 'I mean, not thinking about your mother and stepfather but just about you.'

A small flicker as if from a lamp shone in Howard's eyes.

'No. Oh no, I'd be glad. You can have no idea how awful it is. People looking at you and whispering – everybody whispers. Every time I see somebody whispering I know what they're saying.'

'And what are they?' Patrick asked.

Howard had to force out the answer.

'Howard's washed up.'

The children were furious on Howard's behalf.

'You're crackers,' said Emma. 'You should hear what the girls at our school say about you. They're sloppy over you.'

'And if you think that's what people are going to think when they see you're opening the fête you're bonkers,' Paul went on. 'They'll come in thousands.'

'And all you've got to do is to make a little speech and buy things at the stalls,' Patrick pointed out. 'And policemen will have to hold back the crowds, you'll see.'

But Howard refused to be comforted.

'People won't come, and I can't make a speech, and I've no money to spend at the stalls.'

'No money!' This was the last lunacy. A film star and no money!

'You must have some,' Patrick argued. 'I mean, you're paying a lot to stay with us. Everything nice you're paying for, like this boat and the ponies.'

'I haven't any of my own though,' Howard explained. 'I'm not allowed in shops in case I'm recognised, so anything I want my stepfather pays for me.'

Paul was so annoyed he nearly upset the boat.

'If you ask me, your stepfather's a crook. What you want to do, Howard, is to get the guts to tell him so. Now don't fuss about the fête, we'll write your speech and we'll get Dad to hand over some of your own money so you've plenty to spend.'

'You do what we tell you,' said Emma, 'and we'll make you a different person, a raging lion instead of a scared kitten.'

It was surprising how the holidays turned out after that talk, for making a man of Howard was a hard job. He seemed to have an in-growing humbleness that was terribly difficult to get rid of.

'Don't say "Yes, I'd like to" if you mean "No, I'd hate to,"' Paul told him every day. 'Throw your weight about. Say to yourself "I'm a film star and I'm paying so I can do what I like."'

'Get tough with us as if we were your stepfather,' Emma instructed. 'Say things like "Shut up, it's me who's the star, not you." '

'And do remember,' Patrick implored, 'that everything is yours – your house, your car – no wonder your step-father wants you to go on working.'

And every day they made him wear what they called a 'fête smile'.

'People will expect it,' Emma told him. 'They don't want to see you hang-dog and humble.'

Imperceptibly, even to Howard and the children, this treatment began to work. Howard was still terribly unwilling to put himself forward but he could, after an argument, be made to.

'All right, if you really want me to choose, I'd like to fish. I never have.'

Outwardly, though he did not know it, Howard looked a different boy. He put on weight and he turned a pleasant brown.

'We'll have to have your suits let out,' said Rose, 'and a good thing too, you were far too thin when you arrived.'

This brought out Howard's scared-rabbit look.

'Oh no! There'll be an awful row if I look fat on TV.'

His cousins looked at him sternly.

'We are working very hard on you,' Paul pointed out,

'and we expect results. What you ought to have said was "Who cares about the TV series anyway?"'

But it was the fête that really changed Howard. It exceeded the rector's wildest hopes, for the boy proved to be an enormous draw, almost as big, as Patrick said, as if he was a Beatle. Howard on his own might have forgotten his smile and his confident air, but he never was on his own, one of his cousins was always there to show him off. The little speech they had written for him was a riot.

'I'm not sure who's educating who,' the rector whispered to his wife. 'But it's done our lot no harm to find success is not all it's painted.'

After the fête Howard really began to improve. He never got to the point where he said what he wanted to do before he was asked, but he was able, when there was a choice, to take his part in a family argument. And by degrees a new Howard appeared, a Howard who could be funny, who did not mind telling his cousins all about Hollywood and the stars he had met. A Howard who, now they had stopped being sorry for him, they found that they liked.

'I vote we get Dad to ask Aunt Gena if he can come for Christmas,' Patrick suggested.

'I think it would be a good idea if he came every holidays,' Emma agreed. 'We don't want him becoming hang-dog again and he easily might when we're not there.'

'Too right,' said Paul. 'He's promised to write and say how he gets on, but I wish I could be there to see how his stepfather looks when Howard tells him where he gets off.'

Then suddenly, in the way holidays have, that holiday came to an end. First it was a week before Howard left, then three days, then it was tomorrow. Then today and the family were outside the front door watching Howard drive away. The chauffeur put the luggage in the boot. Paul dug his elbow into Howard's side.

'I'll sit in front,' Howard said in the firm way his cousins had taught him to speak.

The chauffeur looked amused.

'OK. You can slip into the back at the airport.'

Howard knew three pairs of eyes were fixed on him.

'I shall always sit in the front in future. After all it is my car.'

As the Rolls turned out of the gate the children looked proudly at each other.

The rector turned to go into the house.

'For someone who before he came I heard described as "revolting", "loathsome", "hopeless" and "a little beast", I don't think Howard turned out too badly.'

The Quiet Holiday

The Parthan children spent the month of August with their Aunt Phoebe. The custom had started when Jonathan, the eldest, was nine, Alice eight and Patrick seven. That first invitation had arrived in the Easter holidays. The letter was to the children's father.

'The time has come,' Aunt Phoebe had written, 'when you and Araminta must wish to be free of your offspring. If my reckoning is right they have now reached near enough to the age of discretion to be able to visit on their own. If the children do not mind a quiet holiday I shall expect them for the month of August.'

Araminta was the children's mother and she had not been at all sure that at that time her family were ready to visit on their own. Still less when their hostess was her sister-in-law Phoebe, reputed to be very vague.

'All August?' she had said doubtfully. 'Phoebe probably doesn't realise how much looking after and supervision children need.'

The children's father was vicar of a large London parish. He had looked at his wife when she had said this with an amused twinkle in his eye.

'I think Phoebe will do the children good. She is a pretty considerable artist, as you know, and she might teach our little Philistines to look at things with new eyes. And, darling, do you realise it means we can go off on a second honeymoon? It's so long since I had your attention focused on me.'

In the end the children's father had won, so the children had spent that August with Aunt Phoebe. After a rather shaky start it had been a most successful holiday. Aunt Phoebe lived in a little hamlet set in a fold of the Sussex downs. It was the first time the children had met downland and they learned to love it. The short springy turf in which harebells and tiny scabious grew. The chance of finding an arrowhead in the chalk. The dewponds where the earliest shepherds had taken their charges to drink. Above all Martin's Manor. This was an old empty house buried amongst trees like the Princess Aurora's castle. It was during that first summer that the children learned to look upon Martin's Manor as their private property.

The start of that first visit was shaky because as a person Aunt Phoebe took a lot of getting used to. At home in the vicarage the children were planned for and looked after every waking minute, but Aunt Phoebe was appalled by any form of interference, which she considered a deadly sin. So she never told the children when to get up and when to go to bed, or when to wear clean clothes; she never asked where they were going or what they planned to do. To start with the children sat up late and did not bother with baths or teeth or changing their clothes. Quite soon, however, they reverted to the home customs so, though it was without interference, life went on much as usual except that it was spent in glorious Sussex instead of in London.

One reason why the children reverted so soon to home ways was Mrs Wish. Mrs Wish was a roly-poly woman with black hair and eyes bright as a bird's. Mrs Wish came every day to what she called 'do for' Aunt Phoebe. This meant she cleaned the house, cooked the supper and took away what needed washing. While the children were there she provided a cold lunch which she left on the table for them. Mrs Wish did not exactly interfere either but what she said was interfering in her own way. When, at the beginning of their stay, the children stayed up late just because nobody told them to go to bed and as a result came down yawning, late for breakfast, Mrs Wish would greet them with:

'Good afternoon, dears, better late than never I suppose; hope you enjoyed sitting up waiting for Mr Nothing and Mrs Nobody.'

In the non-washing period she would ask:

'Is your neck in mourning for somebody, Jonathan?' or, with a sniff: 'I suppose there are those who would rather be dirty than clean.'

Over clean clothes she didn't hint, she spoke right out:

'There did ought to be three pairs of dirty pyjamas but you've only given me two,' or 'There's no need to wear a dirty shirt, Alice, my washing machine hasn't grumbled yet, I'll tell you when it does.'

Aunt Phoebe was out a great deal working, for she was having a show of her pictures in the autumn, but she was home after tea and then she would have good ideas.

'Why don't we build a bonfire and roast potatoes?' or

'Follow me, we're going to play follow-my-leader.' Then, her red hair blowing in the wind, Aunt Phoebe would lead them on wild capering, dancing, jumping treks across the downs, or she would get out her never-washed old car and say 'Pile in, chickabiddies, let's go and see the moon path across the sea.'

The nicest thing about staying with Aunt Phoebe was a sort of easy feeling. Always at home and at school you seemed to be trying about something or other. To be punctual for meals. Not to fidget in church. To attend at lessons. To please Mummy. Not to disappoint Daddy – there was no end to it. At Aunt Phoebe's you never tried at all, you just sort of let the days slide by.

That first year the children enjoyed themselves without thinking much why they were enjoying themselves, for after all they were only nine, eight and seven. Of course they knew why they enjoyed playing in the grounds of Martin's Manor; who wouldn't enjoy a place so overgrown you had to cut your way like explorers? Which was so secret and so strange that it was easy to be sure you were being chased by bears and seeing Red Indians crawling through the trees.

The next year, to the children's great relief, nothing at Aunt Phoebe's had changed. In the year since they were there it had become a sort of dream place which might have faded. But it hadn't. Aunt Phoebe was just as vague and out just as much though she had not got a picture show that autumn. Mrs Wish was just as bright-eyed and roly-poly as ever and, best of all, Martin's Manor had not changed at all. In fact there were still signs about, like cuts on trees, to show they were still the only inhabitants.

It was the third holiday with Aunt Phoebe when things happened. The year Jonathan was eleven, Alice ten and Patrick nine. When they first arrived everything seemed gloriously as usual. Aunt Phoebe greeted them at the station as she always did, as if she had seen them the day before; she never said how they had grown or asked how they had done at school because she didn't care. There they were – that was all that mattered. The car, when they got into it, looked even more unwashed and old but somehow more splen-did than ever. On the drive to the house Aunt Phoebe told them – as she always did – how busy she was.

'Getting stuff together for a show in New York in the autumn.'

'I say,' said Jonathan, 'that's something like! Are you going over?'

'Flying in September,' Aunt Phoebe said as if flying to America was something everybody did.

Alice, now she was ten, was becoming clothes conscious. Aunt Phoebe always wore green shirts and brown corduroy trousers with a coat to match. If she had any other clothes the children had never seen them. She said cautiously because Aunt Phoebe wouldn't like a direct question:

'Do you have to do a lot of shopping before you go?'

Aunt Phoebe nodded.

'I'm having a suit made. My agent, silly fellow, thinks they only wear skirts in New York, trousers are out; not true of course.' Then she changed the subject to more interesting matters. 'Still some late raspberries going. Mrs Wish has left them on the canes for you to pick.'

'Mrs Wish!' Patrick said contentedly. 'Each year I'm afraid we'll come and she won't be here.'

Aunt Phoebe laughed.

'The day Mrs Wish is not here you won't be here either for I'll be gone too. Couldn't fancy this place without her. No, there are no changes. Though Mrs Wish says there have been a couple of men buying food in the village shop. Camping somewhere I suppose.'

There was nowhere to stay in the hamlet so strangers were always noticed.

Later on the children heard more about the strangers from Mrs Wish.

'Mrs Cotton down at the shop says one or other has been in two or three times. Very close-mouthed they were and she said she didn't care for the look of them. She thinks they're camping on the downs somewhere. I have spoken of them to your auntie but you know what she is so I'm taking it on myself to warn you. Don't none of you run about alone, stick together, that's the best way. I daresay there's no harm in them but you can't be too careful with all the terrible things you read in the papers.'

'Like angel-faced Fabia,' said Alice.

The children did not read the newspapers very carefully but no one could miss the facts about angel-faced Fabia for she was headline news. She was the daughter of a millionaire and had been kidnapped from her school by a gang, so the papers said, who were demanding fifty thousand pounds ransom money. Fabia's father was only too willing to pay the fifty thousand but the kidnappers seemed to have got cold feet and had not turned up to collect the money at the various rendez-vous arranged. 'Angel-faced' was what the newspapers had christened Fabia, though from her photographs the children thought she was not angel-faced at all.

'More horse-faced I'd say,' Patrick had observed.

Alice's mention of angel-faced Fabia made Mrs Wish roar with laughter.

'Well, I wasn't thinking of anybody so terrible as kidnappers, not in these parts, but you be careful like, knock you down for half-a-crown some types would.'

The children were not in the habit of walking about the downs alone so, though they respected anything Mrs Wish said, they didn't think about it much. The only place where they did wander about alone was in the grounds of Martin's Manor and they wouldn't meet anybody there.

As usual the children went to Martin's Manor the morning after they arrived. It was a gloriously unchanging place, only from year to year it got a little more overgrown. Just off what had once been the drive the children had hacked and trodden a track through the tangled rhododendrons, undergrowth and saplings to what they called the garden, for there were some garden trees and shrubs forcing their way up through waist-high weeds. Jonathan led the way, Patrick came next and Alice followed behind. As they walked their eyes were spotting important landmarks: the trees they had marked, the grey squirrel's nest, the place where the foxes lived and the rabbit warren. They walked on tip-toe near the rabbit warren because there were not many rabbits and they tried to keep count of any new ones born since the last summer. They were in luck that morning, the rabbits were out eating and playing.

'Fourteen,' Alice whispered. 'We've never seen fourteen all at once before.'

'That little one with the nice face is quite new,' Patrick breathed.

Jonathan was standing on the top of the warren; now he came back for something extraordinary had caught his attention. The rabbit warren was under a bank and from the top you could just see the manor house – or rather part of it. The roof and the twisted chimneys. It was one of the few places where you could see as much as that for the house was almost hidden by trees. The other two could see from Jonathan's face that he was worried.

'Down,' he whispered.

Puzzled, the other two lay down.

'Why?' asked Patrick.

'What's up?' said Alice.

'Crawl up the bank a bit and look at the chimneys,' Jonathan whispered. 'There's smoke coming out of one. Somebody is inside the house.'

Patrick and Alice crawled up the bank and looked. Jonathan was quite right, there was smoke coming out of the chimney. Very scared, Alice crawled back to Jonathan.

'But there's no way in.'

Jonathan nodded.

'Unless whoever it is broke a window and smashed a shutter.'

Patrick joined the others.

'Let's go and see who it is.'

Jonathan was longing to do just that but he was the eldest and therefore more or less in charge.

'We'll have to go about it carefully, it could be those men Mrs Wish was talking about.'

'If you ask me,' said Alice, 'what we ought to do is to tell Mr Higgs somebody is in the house.'

Mr Higgs was the local policeman, and of course Alice was right but there was a difficulty.

'How can we tell him without telling him we were here?' Jonathan asked. 'I mean in a way it's trespassing.'

It was so long that they had looked on the manor grounds as their own that this was a surprising thought but of course true.

'I vote we creep up and see how they got in,' Patrick suggested, 'and perhaps find out who's inside.'

Jonathan looked at Alice.

'Would you like to wait here until we come back?'

Alice was disgusted.

'Of course not, if you're going to look I'm going to look but do let's be careful.'

Owing to the overgrown state of the grounds there was no difficulty in getting almost up to the house under cover. Arrived, they hid behind a tangle of syringa and lilac trees and studied the house.

Although nobody had lived in Martin's Manor for many years it was not in too bad repair. Every window had been closed and shuttered. Each year a firm of builders came down after the winter and examined the roof for damage and mended anything that needed it, so the children knew there was no way in by lawful means. One careful look at the house and they saw the entrance had not been lawful. There was a small window near the front door. The glass of this had been broken and the shutter cut away.

'I bet whoever did that,' Jonathan whispered, 'got inside and then opened the front door.'

'It must have been a rather small person,' Alice pointed out. 'Nobody big could get in that way.'

This remark of Alice's gave a new angle to the situation. Had children got in? And, if so, what children?

'If it's children,' said Patrick, 'I vote we start a fight.'

But at that moment the front door opened and out

came not a child but a very small man. He was carrying a shopping bag.

Automatically the children tried to make themselves as invisible as possible but they need not have bothered, evidently the man was not worried in case he was being watched. He set off as briskly as was possible across the overgrown grass that had once been a lawn. Then the head of another man looked out through the broken

window. This was a much tougher type. He gave a low whistle.

'Hi, Willie!'

Willie, looking disobliging, turned round.

'What is it?'

The man in the window had a hoarse voice.

'I forgot to say bring a dozen beers.'

'A dozen beers!' said Willie. 'What d'you think I am, Tod, a blooming camel or summat? How can I carry a dozen beers as well as all the other stuff?'

'You'll drink the beer if I know you,' the man in the window retorted. 'Oh – and there's one more thing – ice cream.'

Willie had just started walking again so he was facing the children. He looked so stunned at the mention of ice cream the children wanted to laugh. Indeed nobody could have looked less like an ice cream person than the man in the window.

'Ice cream!' said Willie. Then, a little louder: 'Ice cream!'

The man in the window gave a backwards jerk with his head.

'She won't eat nuffink else. I thought maybe ice cream would tempt her.'

Willie gave an understanding nod.

'Don't want 'er dying on us,' he agreed, and this time he really did get away to do the shopping.

As soon as Willie was out of sight and the man had left the window the children crept further into the undergrowth.

'Are you thinking what I'm thinking?' Alice asked Jonathan.

He nodded.

'I expect so. Mind you, there could be lots of other shes who won't eat.'

Patrick looked from one to the other.

'What are you talking about?'

Jonathan decided to tell him, for Patrick was much easier to deal with if he didn't feel he was being kept out of anything.

'We think there's just a chance that the "she" the men are talking about is angel-faced Fabia.'

'Gosh!' gasped Patrick. 'And we're going to rescue her like knights of old from Willie the Worm and Tod the Terror.'

Both Jonathan and Alice had to giggle at that, the names fitted so beautifully, but then Patrick was good at names. Jonathan said:

'We must get hold of Mr Higgs. I wonder where the nearest telephone is.'

It was about a mile back to the hamlet where there was a telephone booth outside the shop. The children could not imagine one nearer than that.

'If it is angel-faced Fabia,' said Alice, 'I wonder where they've hidden her.'

Jonathan hated them to be divided but there didn't seem any other way.

'One of us must telephone Mr Higgs; we can't say it is angel-faced Fabia, just that it might be and that there are two men.'

Patrick felt sure he was going to be chosen to telephone.

'Mrs Wish says we could all be murdered in our beds before PC Higgs will get a move on.'

'I know he's slow,' Jonathan agreed, 'but he must be told. After all, the best we can do is try to find out where Fabia is hidden; we couldn't rescue her, that's a police job.'

'Who's going to telephone?' Alice asked. 'Shall we draw lots?'

When the children drew lots they used three grasses, bits of stick or whatever was around, and the shortest lost. Jonathan knew all through him this was not a moment for drawing lots, he couldn't leave the others behind while he went to talk on the telephone. The men might look fairly harmless when they were talking about beer and ice cream but they were really desperate characters.

'Why don't you both go?' Jonathan suggested. 'I'll stay here and watch to see if I can get a clue.'

'If we go,' said Alice, 'we'll come back and join you here.'

The important thing was to telephone the police so Jonathan agreed to that.

'Be awfully careful you don't run into Willie. Hide coming out of the gate until you see the road's clear.'

Jonathan, left alone behind the tangle of syringa and old lilac trees, found time passed very slowly. There was no sign of Tod and it seemed as if hours slipped by before he heard feet coming across the lawn. It was Willie returning with the shopping. He now had a second bag which, from the way he sagged to one side, was evidently the beer. Tod had heard him coming and again looked out of the window.

'Taken your time, haven't you?'

Willie put down the bags and mopped his forehead.

'I don't know how I made it, straight I don't, the weight's killing me. You wait, next time it's your turn.'

'You know there won't be a next time if the girl's father wants to see her again.'

'Well, he has tried to pay up,' Willie objected, 'it was us wasn't there.'

'Well, we went, didn't we, but I smelt rozzers. Nobody smells the police quicker than I do.'

'She been carrying on again?' Willie asked.

'No, what I gave her put her out. She won't wake up, not before dinner time. Then she can have the ice cream and I'll put some drops in that.'

Willie picked up the bags.

'Don't overdo it, I don't want to have to dig no grave.'

Jonathan listened, his eyes growing wide with horror. What on earth were the drops they were giving Fabia? And what did Willie mean about graves? He looked at his watch. It was nearly twelve o'clock. What time was the criminals' dinner time?

Both Alice and Patrick were good trackers. They had seen Willie staggering home under the weight of his two bags and had followed a long way behind him. Now, without his hearing a sound, they wriggled into the undergrowth beside Jonathan. Alice whispered:

'Mr Higgs was out at a fire on Mr Seeman's farm, it was Mrs Higgs who told us so we telephoned the farm.'

'He took simply ages coming,' Patrick went on, 'and we couldn't make him understand how desperate it was.'

Alice broke in.

'And he didn't believe us when we said Fabia was perhaps here, he said poachers more like and he'd bicycle up when he had a moment.'

'I shouldn't wonder,' said Patrick, 'if he eats his dinner before he comes.'

'But he is telephoning for help,' Alice reminded Patrick, 'he said he didn't fancy taking on the two of them on his own. I said we'd help but he said "No nonsense now, you cut along home or I'll complain to your auntie."'

Jonathan beckoned to them both to come closer.

'He's drugged her. Tod said she wouldn't come round till dinner time and then he'd put some more drops in her ice cream. Willie told him to be careful as he didn't want to dig a grave.'

This news was so frightening, for a few seconds nobody spoke. Then Alice said in a scared whisper:

'We'll have to get into the house. We can't wait for Mr Higgs.'

'We needn't all go,' said Jonathan. 'One will be enough to warn her about the ice cream.'

Patrick shook his head.

'We've got to find her and when we've found her someone must keep guard, and if it comes to a fight three is better than one.'

'You remember,' Alice whispered, 'that first year we were here we uncovered a grating at the back of the house. You said, Jonathan, you thought it might lead into a cellar. If there is a cellar I bet that's where she is.'

Jonathan thought about this. He remembered the grating because he would have liked to get into the house, only, of course, they couldn't because going into a house was real trespassing, which playing in the grounds was not quite. It certainly was a good idea of Alice's to try it because, even suppose Fabia wasn't there, it might be a way to get to her. He raised himself as high as he dared and peered out. Presently he lowered himself.

'We'll have to go snake-like round the right of the house. There's tons of stuff growing there to hide us, it's not so good on the left. Follow me. When we get round I'll stop for I can't see from here what the cover's like and I may have to recce.'

When you are crawling like a snake through difficult undergrowth, terrified of every twig cracking, even a short distance seems to take hours. When at last Jonathan stopped, Alice and Patrick felt absolutely exhausted.

'Wait here,' Jonathan whispered. 'I'll take a look.' Presently he crawled back. 'It's OK. The cover's not so good but all the windows are shuttered, no one can look out.'

The crawling started again. On and on they went, carefully following where Jonathan led. Grasses tickled their noses; their backs and knees ached, and perspiration blinded them. Then Jonathan stopped so suddenly that Alice, who was behind him, was on top of him. From not far away came a muffled scream followed by a child's voice saying, 'Take it away. I won't eat it.'

They all recognised Tod's voice.

'You'll eat it and like it, my lady. Ice cream fit for a queen that is.'

'I don't want it. I don't want it.' The child's voice persisted but it was clear she was having no chance to refuse the ice cream for her voice became choked and indistinct while Tod shouted:

'Hold her head steady, Willie, or I can't get the stuff in.'

Sick with horror the children listened, powerless to help. Presently the child's voice died away still sleepily protesting.

Then the children heard Willie say:

'She's off again. I don't like the look of her. I do hope you haven't given her too much.'

Tod gave a snort.

'Hark at you! She's all right. We'll leave now and have our dinner. I could do with a drop of beer.'

There were evidently steps from the cellar up into the house proper. The children heard the men climb them, then a door was slammed and locked.

Jonathan had stopped close to the grating. Without discussion the children crawled forward to it and peered down. It was not far to the basement level but when you got there it didn't look as if there was a way in. Jonathan felt round the grating to see if it would lift which, surprisingly, after a little work it did. Cautiously the children moved it until a space was cleared big enough for them to climb down. Then Jonathan lowered first Alice, then Patrick and finally himself.

There was a window into the cellar and miraculously it, of all the windows in the house, was not shuttered; and there was a small hole in it, which was how the children had heard so clearly. But if they were to get in the whole window had to be broken and how did you break glass without being heard? They all knew about fixing it with adhesive tape but of course they had none. They knew, too, you could cut glass with a diamond but they hadn't a diamond either.

Jonathan wrapped his hand in his handkerchief.

'We'll have to risk being heard. It's an old house so I

expect the walls are thick.' He drew back his arm and with all his weight behind him punched the window. The glass fell to the floor with a crash.

The wait after the crash felt endless. The children strained their ears for running feet and shouts but nothing happened. At last Jonathan said:

'We've got away with it. Now we have to pick the rest of the glass out so that we can get in.'

Of course they couldn't pick all the glass out and they didn't want to break any more, it was trying their luck too high. So when they had moved as much as they could they hung their pullovers over the jagged glass and climbed in over them without cutting themselves.

Inside the cellar was dark as night.

'I suppose they use a torch,' Jonathan whispered. 'If only that girl was awake and could make a noise to lead us to her.'

'Hush!' said Alice. 'I think I can hear something.'

They stood still as rocks and presently they heard a sound. A sort of weak moan.

'It's over there,' Alice whispered. 'Let me go first, I'm the quietest and I can almost see in the dark.'

This last wasn't true but Alice had moved so it was too late to argue, and it *was* true that Alice could move quietly. She crawled, feeling her way with her hands.

She was lucky there was nothing on her road and presently she touched something soft. She ran her hands
gently over the something: it was a girl with long hair.

'Come here,' Alice said, 'I've found her. I'm sure it's
angel-faced Fabia. They said she had curly hair and this
girl has.'

The boys joined Alice and they all tried to wake
Fabia but it was no good. She moaned and groaned but
the drops worked, she didn't wake up.

'We'll have to carry her out,' said Jonathan. 'I expect
I could haul her up through the grating and then we'll
have to hide her until Mr Higgs comes. Which I hope
won't be long for they're sure to search for her when
they find she's gone.'

'I'll take her feet,' Patrick offered, 'if you and Alice
can manage the rest of her.'

'Right,' Jonathan agreed. 'Come on, Alice.'

But Alice didn't move.

'Listen!'

They listened.

Alice's ears were sharp. There were steps overhead.

'Quick!' Alice whispered. 'Let's drag her over there
then I'll lie down here. They can only have a torch or
a candle. They mightn't know the difference.'

Jonathan and Patrick dragged Fabia as far as they

could before the cellar door was unlocked and the two men came down.

'Take the torch and go and look for yourself, fusspot,' Tod said. 'The girl's no more dying nor dead than you are.'

Fabia had been lying on a piece of sacking. Alice had lain down in the same place and had buried her face in her arms. Willie, waving the torch, came over to her. At once Alice gave a moan.

'Sounds all right,' said Willie. 'Making noises she is.'

'Like to feel her heart?' Tod asked sarcastically.

'No. She's alive,' Willie agreed. 'How long will she be out?'

Tod considered.

'Hard to say. She didn't take all the ice cream, kept spitting it out. A couple of hours maybe. But that will be enough. We'll be wanting her to walk later, remember.'

Willie went back to Tod.

'Are you sure it's going to work this time and we're really collectin' the fifty thousand?'

'It'll work,' said Tod, 'or else.'

The way he said 'or else' made the children's teeth chatter.

When the men were gone and the door locked the boys came back to Alice.

'Come on. It's going to take all of us to get her up through the grating.'

Alice got up.

'I'll help you get her out but then I'm coming back. Don't you see, as long as they think they've got her here they won't look for her. It's much safer.'

Jonathan had always thought Alice was a good sport but now he was really admiring and so was Patrick.

'Won't you be afraid?' Patrick asked.

'Sort of,' Alice agreed. 'But if they find I'm the wrong girl there wouldn't be any point in killing me.'

'Scream if you are in danger,' said Jonathan. 'Scream like mad. We'll only go to the corner where we can see when Mr Higgs arrives. There's a lot of thick stuff there where we can hide her.'

Alice, having helped get Fabia out from under the grating which, though she was little and thin, was much more difficult than they had supposed, came back to the piece of sacking. She had expected to be terrified but, surprisingly, what she felt was sleepy and she actually did go to sleep. She was woken by Tod and Willie stumping down the stairs. Luckily she remembered where she was and turned over on her face.

Willie hurried to her so she gave a moan to tell him she was alive. Tod handed Willie the torch.

'Hold this. I'll wake her.'

Tod's way of waking a person was rough. First he shook Alice and then he gave her several hard slaps on each cheek, but Willie didn't turn the torch on her so neither man noticed they had the wrong girl.

'It's no good,' Tod said. 'Better get her some coffee. We'll need her perked up if she's to speak on the telephone to her dad.'

'How d'you know once she's on the phone she's only going to say what you tell her?'

Tod gave a nasty laugh.

'Would you say anything you shouldn't with a gun in your earhole?'

Willie made a shuddering noise.

'Oh dear, I do hate guns! I do wish you wouldn't carry one. You can be as rough as you like without using a gun.'

Alice, who Tod had thrown back on to the piece of sacking, also hated the thought of Tod carrying a gun. To take her mind off it she thought hard about Fabia. Had the boys managed to hide her safely? When, oh when would Mr Higgs come?

Help was much nearer than Alice could imagine. Mr Higgs might be considered slow by Mrs Wish, and in a way he was, but when he had properly digested facts his mind worked well. While he was keeping sightseers away from the fire and the traffic moving he was digest-ing what Alice had told him on the telephone. As a result of his thinking and as soon as the fire brigade had the fire under control he went to the farmhouse and made a telephone call. The result of that call was that Jonathan and Patrick were startled to see eight policemen, including Mr Higgs, one with an Alsatian dog, quietly approaching the house.

Patrick would have forgotten caution and rushed out to meet them but Jonathan, remembering there might be a face at the broken window, restrained him.

'You can go to Mr Higgs but keep under cover. Explain we've got Fabia and about where Alice is.'

That was how, a few minutes later, Alice was sure she heard a sound outside the cellar window. It was in fact the first constable climbing through.

'What was that?' said Tod. 'I'm sure I heard some-thing.'

'So did I,' Willie agreed. 'We better run for it.'

'Not without her I don't,' said Tod, and he picked up Alice as if she was a sack of potatoes and flung her over his shoulder. Willie was already climbing the stairs.

'Come on, do.'

A fierce light from a torch was turned on Tod and Alice.

'It's no good running anywhere. We've got you cov-
ered.'

And the police had. Four of them were outside the
door of the cellar, three, including Mr Higgs, were in
the cellar and the one with the Alsatian was waiting by
the grating in case either man tried to escape.

And that was the end really. An ambulance took
Fabia to the hospital and the children were driven
home in a police car.

'Please don't tell our Aunt Phoebe what happened,'
Jonathan begged Mr Higgs. 'She doesn't like interference and if people know they might bother her with
questions.'

The policemen all laughed at that.

'We can't keep this a secret,' Mr Higgs explained. 'If
I know anything you'll have reporters and cameras all
round the house by this evening.'

That was exactly what happened. The children even
had to appear on TV and their faces were on the front
page of every paper. The excitement went on for weeks,
long after the children were back in the vicarage.

In the spring Aunt Phoebe wrote a letter.

'I'll expect the children in August as usual, that is,
unless they are staying with their millionaire friends' –
this was because Fabia's father had taken them all

winter-sporting in Switzerland in the Christmas holidays, just one of his many presents to them – 'But this year I must make a stipulation. They will please do nothing to attract attention. They are invited for just a quiet holiday.'

Roberta

Roberta's home was in Hollywood. Her father was English and her mother a Scot. They lived in Hollywood because Roberta's father was a film director. Roberta's mother was delicate, so, as she was not often well enough to drive her to school, her father had arranged that Roberta should attend the studio school.

The arrangement might be convenient but it was not a good one for Roberta. The pupils in a studio school are those children who are under contract to the studio. When Roberta attended the school, though a few of the children were small-part or stand-in actors, there were several really clever child stars. Lots of children would have enjoyed going to a studio school to work with child stars, but not Roberta, for it made her feel inferior. To counteract this feeling, whenever she got a chance, Roberta bragged, usually about things that had not really happened but would have made her feel grand if they had.

When Roberta was eleven her life changed. She heard about it one morning when she and her father were driving to the studio.

'The doctor wants Mummy to winter in the mountains, so I'm taking her to Switzerland.'

'Switzerland!' Roberta was surprised. 'But there are mountains here.'

'That's what I was coming to.' Her father was clearly feeling for the right words. 'Mummy and I think it's time you knew Mummy's country. So after I've settled her in Switzerland I am taking you to Britain. You're to spend the winter with Mummy's mother – your grandmother.'

Roberta was so surprised she felt dizzy.

'Grandmother! Will I like that?'

Her father was amused.

'I hope so. But even if you don't it will do you a power of good, you've been in this hot-house atmosphere since

you were eight, so Mummy and I think Scotland might
be just what you need.'

After that things moved so fast that Roberta felt like
a kitten trying to catch its tail. Having left her mother
in Switzerland she was brought by her father to London,
where she stayed three days for shopping.

'You've got to have some clothes. We're meeting a lady
who'll take you shopping.'

'What sort of clothes am I to buy?'

Her father took a list from his notebook.

'Mummy's written it out.'

Roberta took the list and read it.

One tweed overcoat.
One tweed coat and skirt.
Three twin sets.
Two well-cut but simple dresses suitable for
    parties where games are played.
One real party frock.

'What's the party frock for?'

'Your grandmother was a great harp player. The
car smash which killed your grandfather injured her
right arm. She has not been able to play the harp
since. But she still gives her big November musical

party as she always did, only other people play at it
now.'

Roberta's father was going to stay with his father and
mother before he went back to Switzerland so Roberta
travelled to Edinburgh in charge of the guard, and her
grandmother met her at the station. Grandmother's
home was a shock to Roberta. Instead of the magnificent castle, such as Scots lived in on the movies, it was
a flat in a gaunt, grey square. But Grandmother herself
was not a disappointment. In fact, from the moment
she saw her, Roberta admired her enormously and
longed for Grandmother to admire her. Certainly her
grandmother was most distinguished-looking in an indi-
vidual way. Having been a well-known figure she had
become a law unto herself, caring nothing for fashion, so
sweeping about in elegant dresses she designed herself.
Unfortunately, though Roberta admired her grandmother, her grandmother was less happy about Roberta
for, from their first meal together, Roberta, hoping to be
liked, lied in order to impress her.

'Our teacher at the studio school said I was an un-
usually musical child. I said I expected I inherited it
from you.'

Grandmother was surprised, not having heard music
mentioned in connection with Roberta.

'Indeed! What instruments are you studying?'

'Not exactly any instrument, just generally musical. You know.'

'I'm afraid I do not. Now tell me, dear, about yourself, what are your hobbies?'

Roberta had no particular hobby, or rather she had a new one every week which, if she had explained, her grandmother would have understood. Instead she chose the hobby likely to be approved.

'Reading. I read nearly every book in our school library.'

Grandmother was delighted.

'Good. That gives us a lot in common.'

But after a very short book talk Grandmother could see Roberta had not told the truth and she felt sad and disappointed, while Roberta felt miserable because Grandmother, whom she was trying so hard to please, became cold and distant.

And that was how things went on. Roberta could not see that all Grandmother wanted was her real grand-child. To make things worse Roberta found at the school to which she was sent that she was way behind the other girls at work, so was made to do lessons in a class with children of nine. This made her feel humiliated, but instead of trying to change things by working extra hard she struggled to impress the other girls by bragging about all the stars she had met in Hollywood, and by talking with a phoney American accent. At first the girls were interested and in playtime Roberta had a crowd round her, but soon the novelty wore off.

'Oh, that Roberta!' they groaned to each other. 'She hasn't a thought in her head except about film stars.'

Roberta was not insensitive so soon she knew she was not a success. Often she cried herself to sleep.

'They're all hateful in Scotland. Nobody likes me.'

Then one day in November, five days before her own party, Grandmother had a letter.

'An old friend, a Mrs MacGregor, is giving a party on Saturday, it's for her daughter Sarah. You are invited, Roberta.'

Roberta's face had become rather sad-looking, but at the thought of a party it lit up as if there was a lamp in her head.

'Oh goody! I'm so sick of plain clothes.'

'I'm afraid this will not be a dressing-up party. For that you must wait for my evening party next Thursday.' She turned back to her letter. 'Mrs MacGregor says: "Sarah's latest craze is a game called Murder, which can be rough, so please send Roberta in old things." You have that nice brown frock, it will do capitally.'

Roberta said, 'Yes, Grandmother,' but inside she was

protesting for she loathed woollen clothes. 'I won't tell
Grandmother,' she thought, 'but I won't go to a party in
brown wool. I absolutely won't.'

But when she was in her bedroom looking through
her clothes it seemed as if Grandmother's idea was right,
for the only alternative to the brown wool was a char-
coal wool. It was then Roberta had her great idea. The
MacGregors had never seen her. Now was her chance
to impress somebody. No matter what the letter said she
would wear her grand party dress. What an entrance she
would make with all the other guests dressed in wool!
'Who is that lovely child?' the grown-ups would whisper,
and soon everybody would be telling each other that she
came from Hollywood so no wonder she looked different.

On the Saturday Roberta was so full of the vision of
herself arriving in her party frock that she found it hard
to hide from Grandmother how excited she was feeling.
Grandmother noticed that Roberta looked much more
gay than usual and she was glad.

'A taxi is coming for you at a quarter to three. I wish
I could go with you but I have to go to Glasgow to see
somebody about my party.' She hesitated. 'If I tell you a
secret will you promise to tell nobody?'

Roberta could not imagine a secret of Grandmother's
she would want to tell anybody.

'Of course.'

'It is Yehudi Menuhin* I am seeing. He is up here for some concerts. It is just possible he will play at my party.'

'Yehudi Menuhin!' Roberta gasped. One of the greatest artists in the world perhaps coming to Grandmother's house. What a thing to tell them about at school! Even the senior girls would like to talk to somebody who had talked to Yehudi Menuhin.

'How gorgeous! Oh, I do hope he comes.'

'So do I,' Grandmother agreed briskly, for she hated what she called sloppiness. 'But it is unfortunate my appointment with him is today for I should like to have introduced you to the MacGregors.'

'Thank goodness you can't,' thought Roberta, with a pleased shiver at the picture of the sensation she was going to cause that afternoon.

Grandmother went out immediately after lunch, and waiting only to be sure Mrs Donald, the daily, was safely in the kitchen, Roberta rushed to her room to put on the party dress.

It was a charming frock, a bit little-girlish for Roberta's taste but undeniably pretty. It was white with

---

* Yehudi Menuhin is widely considered to have been one of the greatest violinists of the twentieth century.

sticking-out skirts, it had little roses sprinkled over it and rose-coloured slippers. When she was dressed Roberta could not leave her looking-glass.

But at the MacGregors' house Roberta felt less confident. She arrived at the same time as the other guests and was dismayed to find most of them she knew, for they went to her school. In the bedroom into which they were shown to remove their coats Roberta shrank against a wall, unwilling to take off her tweed coat while the others were looking, for she certainly was going to be conspicuous.

'Come on, Roberta,' a girl called Peggy said, giving a pull at Roberta's coat. 'We're going down now.'

'Shan't be a minute,' said Roberta. 'You go on.'

The girls went on but downstairs they gathered in groups round Peggy, who was telling Sarah about Roberta.

'I'm almost sure she's dressed for a dance. I swear I saw silk when I pulled her coat.'

'She can't be,' Sarah protested. 'I know Mummy told her grandmother she wasn't to dress up.'

'You don't know our Roberta,' the girls from the school said. 'She's an awful show-off.'

Sarah was well brought up.

'Whatever she's got on none of you is to say anything.

It's my party and I won't have her made to feel embarrassed.'

Though nobody said a word Roberta did feel embarrassed, for instead of the buzz of admiration she'd expected nobody paid any attention to her. Inside she knew she had made a mistake and she was miserable. Sarah came to her rescue.

'We're starting with hide-and-seek. All the curtains are drawn and I'm putting out the lights. You can hide anywhere in the house.'

In the blessed dark Roberta stopped feeling self-conscious and ran up the stairs and hid behind some curtains. The seeker was a boy and presently Roberta heard him coming up the stairs. Then he was fumbling at the curtains. In the dark unseen hands were frightening so, just as the boy was about to touch her, Roberta could bear no more. She gave a shriek and dashed down the stairs. But the boy was too quick for her, he caught her by the skirt. There was a dreadful ripping noise and the frock tore from the waist.

Sarah took Roberta to her mother.

'Oh, my dear child!' Mrs MacGregor said in dismay. 'Why did your grandmother let you wear this lovely frock? This isn't just a mending matter, the silk's torn.'

Roberta was nearly crying.

'Grandmother doesn't know I'm wearing it.'

'Then why did you?'

Mrs MacGregor seemed kind and understanding.

'Nobody notices me in Scotland. I feel inferior.'

Mrs MacGregor gave Roberta a kiss.

'Bless the child! Inferior indeed! Now you take that off and put on something of Sarah's.' She put an arm round Roberta. 'Try not to worry, it will spoil your fun.'

Mrs MacGregor rang Grandmother on the telephone, so when Roberta got home she already knew what had happened.

'Take off your coat and let me see the damage.'

Roberta took off her coat and turned her back to Grandmother. She had been tacked together but the damage was plain to see. Grandmother made worried, clucking sounds with her tongue against her teeth.

'This is the only frock you have for an evening party?' Roberta nodded. Grandmother gently turned her round. 'Then I'm afraid you won't be able to be present at my party. Such a pity, for Yehudi Menuhin is going to play.'

Grandmother's party had been talked about so much, to miss it was dreadful enough, but to miss meeting Yehudi Menuhin was unbearable.

'Oh please! I'm sure I can mend it.'

Grandmother had seen Roberta's attempts at sewing.

'I doubt if I could so you could not.'

Roberta felt as if she would never smile again. Tears trickled down her cheeks.

'I wanted to be somebody. It's awful being despised. The other girls look down on me. I can't dance reels like they do, and I'm not much good at lessons. And you despise me – so I thought ...'

Roberta was not looking at Grandmother or she would have seen a very sorry expression on her face.

'Give me a kiss, dear, and then you must go to bed. Tomorrow I'll have another look at the frock and see what can be done.'

But by the next morning it was Roberta who knew what must be done. It seemed as if tearing the frock had done something to her, for she knew how silly she had always been. When she came down to breakfast she kissed Grandmother but, instead of sitting, stood by her chair.

'I don't think the frock could be mended by Thursday, but I've got another idea.'

'And what is that?'

'You said caterers come in to do the food. Couldn't I wear an apron and help hand round?'

'I think my friends might think I was unkind to my granddaughter if I dressed her in an apron.'

Roberta shook her head.

'You needn't say I'm your granddaughter. I just want to be there so I can see everybody, especially Yehudi Menuhin.'

Grandmother put an arm round Roberta.

'I too have been thinking about the frock and an apron may not be necessary. In a way I'm grateful that the dress got torn, for a granddaughter who is contented to stay in the background wearing an apron is the sort of granddaughter I know that someday I am going to be very proud of.'

Green Silk

Emma did not know where she was at first. It was very dark, but she seemed to be in some sort of barn, the type where, on farms, everything was kept that was not being used that very minute. She raised herself on her elbow. She was lying on some sacks that had been thrown on to some straw. It was the straw that brought yesterday rushing back. There was a pile of the stuff outside and she could remember picking up some armloads and tossing them into the barn to make a bed, then throwing herself down on it and crying until she supposed she had fallen asleep.

Emma went to the door and peered out. She wondered what the time was for she had forgotten to wind her watch last night. Nobody was about but it must, she thought, be very early in the morning, for it was only just beginning to be light. A church clock sounded; she counted the strokes, it was six o'clock. Six o'clock! No wonder she was hungry. She had not eaten anything since breakfast yesterday. Cautiously Emma stepped outside and took her bearings. The barn she had slept in was part of a group of outhouses. She peered through a hedge and saw quite a large farmhouse and near it something that made her hungry inside turn over: a hen-house and, to make sure she knew it was a hen-house, a cock crowed. Hens! Would it be a dreadful sin to take an egg? It would be, of course, a sort of stealing, only when you were what was called 'on the run' didn't taking an egg stop being stealing and become 'living off the land', which sounded so much more respectable?

The worst of being really hungry is that seeing food makes you drool. Emma discovered she had lost her handkerchief so she had to wipe her mouth on the back of her hand. Then she crept forward across the garden. It was, she was certain, a foolhardy thing to do for she had heard farmers got up awfully early, but the longer she left it the more certain she was to be caught.

The hens, like many human beings, did not like to be woken suddenly. They liked to be awake and ready to get more than their share of breakfast when they were let out of the hen-house. So when they felt Emma's cold hungry fingers fumbling underneath them, they at once broke into indignant, noisy, enraged cacklings. Emma had got herself into the hen-house with difficulty and was not to be put off by cackles.

'Oh, do shut up, hens,' she said. 'I'm sorry to disturb you but I do need an egg.' She stopped there for she was interrupted by a giggle.

Then a voice said, 'Sorry to disturb you, but why must you have one of our eggs?'

Emma straightened up and turned to find herself face to face with a boy who looked as though he had got straight out of bed, unwashed and unbrushed, and had put on the first clothes that came to hand. Then she remembered she was in no condition to criticise. Her school uniform must look awful after being slept in and it was hours since she had last washed.

'I'm sorry, but I am so hungry, and it wasn't stealing, at least I thought it wasn't because I'm on the run so I have to live off the land ... '

The boy came round to the back of the hen-house and let out the hens.

'I don't think they've laid yet. But if you come to the house I'll give you something to eat.'

He scattered the chickens' breakfast, which he was carrying, and led the way to the house.

'You'll have to be quiet,' he warned. 'The parents don't get up until seven and they'll take a dim view if you wake them earlier.'

'Especially as all you know about me is I was trying to steal an egg,' said Emma.

The boy glanced at her. She looked a mess. They were near the house so they spoke in a whisper.

'Have you ever stolen eggs before?'

Emma was shocked. She must, of course, be looking scruffy, but did she look scruffy enough to be a regular thief?'

'No,' she whispered. 'I certainly have not.'

In the kitchen the boy found some bread and a big piece of cheese and an apple.

'You'd better take that with you. I'm going mushrooming and I can't leave you here.'

It was a nice kitchen, the sort in which people eat as well as cook. It had, Emma noticed, everything anyone could want, such as a deep-freeze and heaps of gadgets and plastic bags. Very unlike her kitchen at home which was modelled on the canteens where her parents, who were lecturers, ate most of their meals. She tore a plastic bag off a roll of them fastened to the wall and packed up the bread and cheese and the apple.

'Could I borrow a knife?' she whispered.

The boy nodded. He had collected a large basket. 'Come on, let's go.'

Away from the house Emma said, pointing, 'I spent the night in there. Could I go there to eat my breakfast?'

The boy considered. 'Better not. Dad will be down soon and if he finds you there'll be no end of explaining to do. Make a sandwich to eat on the way and keep the rest until you get there.'

A tree had been cut down. It made quite a good table. Emma sawed off a thick slice of bread and put a wedge of cheese on it.

'Get where?' she asked.

'Where the mushrooms grow of course. But you mustn't tell anyone where we got them or they'll swipe the lot.'

It was a lovely walk to the mushroom field – or would have been to anyone not blinded by self-pity. They walked along a path by a small river from which a mist was rising, so it looked as if everything was shrouded in lace. The moment the first piece of bread and cheese and apple were eaten, Emma sat down on the path and cut another sandwich. Even feeling miserable she knew it was the most gorgeous breakfast she had ever eaten.

Presently they left the river and turned into a wood. The wood was quite large and ended with a gate which had a padlock on it and a board which read: 'Trespassers will be prosecuted'. On the other side of the gate were mushrooms. Emma climbed over the gate without saying a word, but she gave the boy a look to show she felt they were now equals in crime.

The boy said, 'This field belongs to my father.'

'Oh yes,' Emma replied in a tone which showed she did not believe a word of it.

Of all things you can pick, mushrooms are some of the best. It's true you have got to kneel or bend double or sit on the ground to get at them, but once you have, what else grows in an obliging ring, so that even if a mushroom is still pushing its way out fingers will find it?

Emma had quite a job not to enjoy herself, but to remain focused on her troubles. She was putting her mushrooms in the plastic bag now empty of bread and cheese. So she and the boy had drifted apart. 'When the bag's full,' the boy had said, 'tip your mushrooms into my basket.'

The bag was quite big so it took time to fill it, which meant that Emma, turning over her sorrows in her mind, reduced herself to tears, so many tears that she lay face down inside a mushroom ring where she could get the sobs out of her system.

It was at the height of her sobbing that the boy rejoined her. He wondered at first if it would be best to pretend not to notice, but soon he realised that was impossible. Her face had been smudged with past tears when he had first seen her, now it must look like a Guy Fawkes. While he was deciding what to do he tipped her mushrooms out of the bag into his basket. He was tempted to go away then, there were still dozens of mushrooms to be picked worth no end of money at the price wild mushrooms were fetching, but he was a kind boy. Perhaps he ought to ask if anything was wrong, though he did not suppose it was like someone being dead or she wouldn't have been able to wolf that bread and cheese as she had.

'I say,' he asked, 'what's up?'

Emma checked her sobs.

'I'm running away because everything's come to an end for me.'

The boy was practical. He liked to get his facts straight.

'When did you start to run away?'

Emma spoke between sobs but they were getting less. 'Yesterday morning.'

'Where did you run from?'

'My school.'

'Why? I mean something must have happened.'

The boy saw he had reached the sore spot. Emma was now sitting up and a proper sight she looked, red, swollen, wet and now more tears. It did seem as though something really terrible had happened, like when a boy at his school was run over by a bus. Regretfully he gave up the idea of picking the rest of the mushrooms, perhaps he'd be lucky and find them still there tomorrow.

'You haven't a handkerchief, have you?' Emma gulped. 'I lost mine yesterday.'

The boy produced a deplorable grey object and passed it to her.

'Come on, nobody runs away for nothing.'

Emma blew her nose and struggled to speak clearly. 'I might have been a bridesmaid but I couldn't be because Dad and Mum would be in America, and they sent me to France. Imagine France when you might have been a bridesmaid!'

The boy was hopelessly muddled. 'But when was the wedding?'

'Weeks ago and the bridesmaid wore green silk.'

'But if it was weeks ago why run away yesterday?'

Emma took a deep breath and swallowed her last sob. 'I'll begin at the beginning.'

The boy felt it might be a long story. 'Come along. Tell me on the way back. I'm starving.'

Emma began the moment they were over the stile. 'Dad and Mum came home this summer to fix things up so they could stay in America another year and they hoped to go to Aunt Madge's wedding in Scotland. Aunt Madge is Mum's much younger sister, but the dates were wrong so I couldn't be a bridesmaid because there was no one to take me to Scotland.'

The boy interrupted, hoping to shorten the story. 'Why couldn't you go alone?'

'Dad and Mum said no I couldn't but that wasn't why I ran away. It was because of what I heard.'

The boy paused to pick a blackberry. 'What did you hear?'

'I've got a cousin at my school, she's called Prunella and she's Aunt Pat's child. I had just finished unpacking and so I went into the garden. Prunella was talking in a whisper to another girl so I wondered why she was whispering.'

'And you listened in?'

Emma had the decency to blush. 'Well, there was a tree and I got behind it.'

The boy longed to say that people who listened in on somebody else's conversation never heard good of themselves, but he didn't want to risk Emma crying again so he merely nodded to show he was listening.

Emma felt a lump grow in her throat so she quickly swallowed it.

'Prunella was talking about Aunt Madge's wedding. I was never to know, she said, but she had been the bridesmaid instead of me. She said it was all a wangle because Aunt Madge didn't want Emma – that's me. What Prunella said Aunt Madge said was: "Oh, not Emma! That girl with all those spots and that figure would ruin the wedding. Get them to keep her in France until it's over."'

The boy looked at Emma. Certainly she did look pretty terrible now, not a bit like the bridesmaids at the only wedding he had been to. Still, dolled up in green silk, perhaps she'd look better.

'So you didn't run away from your school?'

'No, I ran away because I won't go to half term and things with Aunt Pat who sneaked Prunella up to Scotland when it should have been me.'

They were getting near the farm. The boy said, 'You'd better come in and tell Dad and Mum where you have come from. I should think the school's gone mad by now and there are police hunting for you everywhere.'

This time they went in at the front door into the dining room. The boy's mother and father were eating porridge. They both stopped eating to look at Emma. Then the boy's father asked, 'Is your name Emma?'

Emma nodded.

The man got up. 'I'll ring the police.'

The boy's mother said, 'Sit down and have some breakfast. Get a plate and an extra cup, David.'

There are, as everyone knows, all types of grown-ups. David's proved to be the best kind. His father was a long time on the telephone, and meanwhile Emma ate two plates of porridge with cream, and four rashers of bacon and an egg, and told David's mother her sad story, this time without tears, and almost without a lump in her throat, but not quite for, after all, there is nothing funny about being cheated out of being a bridesmaid. David's mum was a grand listener and her face showed how sorry she was. At the end she said, 'I can't imagine why they couldn't have had both you and Prunella as bridesmaids.'

Emma was amazed. 'With my spots and looking like I look!'

David's mother dismissed that. 'Everybody goes

through spotty patches, it's part of growing up. A little make-up would have hidden them.'

'Aunt Madge had always said she would only have one big bridesmaid,' Emma explained. 'There were six tiny ones.'

David's father came back. 'You haven't half put the cat among the pigeons, young woman. It seems half the police in the county have been out searching for you all night.'

'Does she have to go back at once?' David asked, 'or could I show her the stables?'

David's father gave his mother a look to show he wanted to talk to her so she said the stables were a good idea.

Left alone,' he said, 'They won't have Emma back at The Old Manor School. I talked to the head who sounded a dragon. She said if we brought Emma back this morning she could go up into the sanatorium, and stay there until her parents in America made other arrangements for her. Under no circumstances would she take back a girl who ran away. I nearly asked her if she was afraid Emma would set a fashion.'

'Thank goodness you didn't,' said David's mother, 'because I've got an idea. I've taken a fancy to Emma – of course she's been silly, but what child isn't at times, and she was provoked. You said you'd try and get a boy to work with David at the stables. Why not have Emma instead? I always wanted a daughter.'

David's father caught the idea at once. 'And she could go to the Comprehensive with David. I wonder if her parents would mind. I've got the name and address of her Aunt Pat, who seems to be married to a man I know. It shouldn't be difficult to arrange.'

On the way to the stables Emma had learned that David's father hadn't a proper farm, he dealt in horses – mostly trained other people's race horses – and how David worked as a stable lad on Saturdays and Sundays and all through the holidays. He was hoping to be a jockey when he left school. Emma did not know much about horses but it looked to her as if David had a gorgeous life.

Emma never knew how it all happened. But by that evening she went to bed in her own room feeling one of David's family. She had spoken to her mother and father on the phone and they had said she was an ass to have run away, but all was well that ended well. Thank goodness there was a place for her in the Comprehensive when the term started next week.

When David's mother came in to say good night Emma flung her arms round her neck. 'I can never, never thank you.'

David's mother gave her a kiss. 'Oh yes, you can. There will be plenty of ways but I want one promise as a start. Never, never again, whatever awful thing happens to you, feel sorry for yourself. There is never an excuse for that.'

First Publication Details

'Devon Mettle' published in *The Queen* (January 1933)

'Chicken for Supper' published in *BBC Children's Hour Annual* (1951)

'Flag's Circus' published in *I Spy Annual* (1954)

'The Secret' published in *Noel Streatfeild's Ballet Annual* (1959). This was adapted from a longer version of the story, published as 'The Understudy' in *The Children's Own Treasure Book* (Odhams Press, 1947)

'Coralie' and 'Ordinary Me' published in *Noel Streatfeild's Ballet Annual* (1959)

'Howard' published in *Miscellany Three* (Oxford University Press, 1966)

'The Quiet Holiday' published in *Winter's Tales for Children 4* (Macmillan, 1968)

'The Plain One' published in *Puffin's Pleasure* (Puffin Books, 1976)

'Green Silk' published in *The Noel Streatfeild Weekend Story Book* (Dent, 1977)

We are unable to find publication details of the following stories, but the manuscripts are marked as follows: 'Andrew's Trout' and 'Let's Go Coaching', 1964; 'Cows Eat Flowers', 1965.

We cannot find any publication or date details for 'Roberta' or 'The Old Fool'.